THE SHOP AROUND THE CORNER

A SWEET, SMALL TOWN SOUTHERN ROMANCE

SWEET TEA AND A SOUTHERN GENTLEMAN
BOOK 2

ANNE-MARIE MEYER

SWEET ESCAPE PUBLISHING, LLC

Your person. They come into your life and change everything. You are no longer the person of your past, and you have no idea who future you is either. If your person is with you, you know you'll be safe. But if they aren't, you are so fundamentally changed that you're scared of moving forward without them. He's your life-altering person.

TITAN

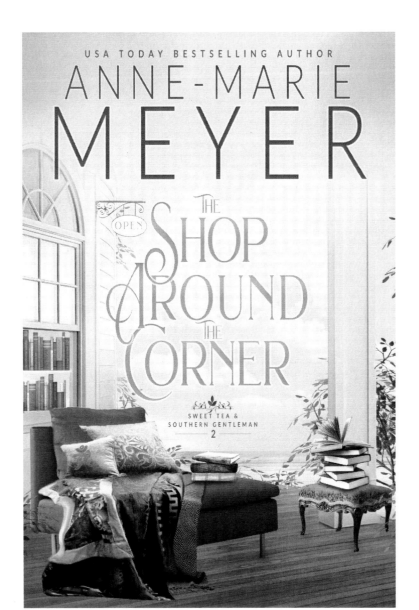

USA TODAY BESTSELLING AUTHOR

ANNE-MARIE
MEYER

THE SHOP AROUND THE CORNER

SWEET TEA &
SOUTHERN GENTLEMAN
2

Dedicated to Margaret Brown
Born 13th May 1961. Died 8th October 2022 age 61
She was such a strong, inspirational woman who had
cancer in nearly every part of her body but she showed no
defeat.
She got up each day and faced the day
Thank you for loving my books.

SHELBY

SWEET TEA &
SOUTHERN GENTLEMAN

I REMEMBER the excitement I felt.

I remember hugging Gran's legs as Mom raced around the house, straightening the pillows and furniture, and dusting ledges for the millionth time that day.

I remember the smell of exhaust when Mr. Lachlan came pulling into the driveway. Mom had Gran and I stand in the grass next to the asphalt like we were some Regency family greeting their guests.

I remember the first time I saw Mr. Lachlan. He was tall with dark hair and dark eyes. He barely looked at me when he walked past.

I remember Miles.

He was small back then. His dirty-blonde hair was tousled and he had chocolate smeared across his cheek.

I remember the wedding. Mom was so happy. Mr.

Lachlan hadn't changed. He was still the cold, hardened man he'd been the first day I met him.

And then he was gone, leaving Miles behind.

I remember Mom's tears after every phone call.

I remember the sound of her wine glass as it hit the cold, marble countertop over and over and over again.

I remember Mom's screams when the alcohol finally kicked in.

I remember the rage in her eyes when she saw me. The distain in her tone as she staggered toward me with her hand raised. The vile words she spewed my direction. That I was the reason for her loneliness. That every man left her because they hated me.

I remember the feeling of her nails across my cheek after she struck me.

I remember the headache I would nurse as I lay there on the floor after she passed out on the couch.

I remember Miles helping me up and into the bathroom where he would gingerly wipe the blood from my lip.

And I will never forget the night Mom grabbed a knife. The glinting metal shone in the darkness.

I stood there, frozen to the spot. Fearing what would happen when she closed the gap between us. I remember knowing I was going to die that night...until I felt a hand grab mine.

I remember my feet moving faster than I thought they

could as I was pulled through the house. When we got to the guest closet, Miles pulled me inside.

And he held me as we listened to my mother's drunken screams as she stumbled through the house looking for me.

Miles pulled me deeper into the discarded blankets and clothes, shielding me with his body.

I remember waking up the next morning.

I remember Gran pulling into the driveway and rushing to our side.

I remember her speaking to the police officer in hushed tones.

I remember Gran ushering us to her car and telling us that we were going to live with her now.

I remember driving away from Mom's house, the only time I saw her after was at her funeral my senior year of high school.

I remember when Gran pulled down Whipporwillow Lane and into the wraparound driveway.

I remember this was the start of the rest of my life at Harmony Island Inn.

1

MILES

SHELBY WAS IN MY BED.

I lay there with her curled up next to me. I could hear her soft breaths and feel her heart pounding a slow and rhythmic beat against my arm. Her hand was resting on my chest and her thigh was burning a spot on my leg that I was certain would scar me forever.

I stared up at the darkness that filled my room. I cursed the feelings that were rushing through me. I'd thought I would be able to sleep with her next to me...I was wrong.

It was taking all of my strength not to touch her. To feel her. To pull her into my arms and show her all the ways a man could please a woman.

I wanted to share that with her. I wanted her to be mine.

But I knew it was too soon for that. She wasn't ready.

She needed to heal.

It wasn't lost on me that after my declaration of love last night, she didn't respond with the same sentiment. I witnessed her feelings for me in the way she kissed me, touched me...stared at me. But she never uttered those three little words.

The words that I'd given so freely.

I love you.

I closed my eyes as my fingers found her hand resting on my chest. I squeezed it gently before bringing it up to my lips. "I love you," I whispered into her knuckles.

My hand engulfed hers as I set it back down on my chest and held it there. My heart was pounding so hard, I could feel its reverberation in my chest. Then I turned to look at her. Her soft brown hair was pulled away from her face, revealing the creamy skin on her neck and jawline. Memories of pressing my lips to those spots flooded my mind. Deep in my stomach, the desire to kiss every part of her came roaring back to life.

I dragged my gaze away from the hollows of her neck to focus on her perfect features. Her eyelashes splayed across her cheeks, the dark brown contrasting against her white skin. Her nose was pointed and perfect. I leaned in and placed a soft kiss on the tip, and when I pulled back, my gaze dropped to her lips. I knew I should look away, but I couldn't help but stare at her plump, pink lips and fantasize about what I would do to them. They were beckoning me to trace their outline with my fingertips and tease them open with my tongue.

I blew out my breath, thankful that she was asleep so she wouldn't witness my torture. Her mouth was relaxed, which only enhanced her beauty. She wasn't frowning— which I'd grown so accustomed to—but she wasn't smiling. She looked content.

So content that I forced myself to lie back down on my pillow and slam my eyes shut. I knew kissing her on the lips would wake her up, and even though every molecule in my body was screaming at me to press my lips to hers, I remained still.

Heat burned in my body from desire. I wanted her in ways that I'd never wanted another woman before. Even with Tamara. Even with random girls that used to fill my calendar when I was single and searching. None of them held a candle to how I felt for Shelby.

She was my person. I was made to love her. I was made to make love to her. I was hers, physically, spiritually, emotionally.

My soul yearned to make her mine.

Sleep evaded me. By the time my room began to grow lighter from the waking sun, I was ready to get out of the bed. The temptation to touch Shelby had grown too strong, and I needed to get some distance between us if I was going to hold to my promise to wait until she was ready.

I pulled away from her, slipping my body off the side

of the bed until I was crouching on the floor. A sigh escaped her lips, turning the fire in my belly into a raging inferno. I wanted to pull the covers back and crawl in next to her, but I didn't.

Instead, I stood and stared down at her for a moment, memorizing every part of her face while I had the chance, then turned and headed out of the room.

Belle wouldn't be up yet, so I grabbed the baby monitor and headed out to the garage to work off all the pent-up energy I had inside of me.

My earbuds blared my music as I loaded my weights. I was going heavier than I had in a long time, but with the way I was feeling toward Shelby, my muscles needed to burn.

Sweat dripped down my face as I returned the bar to its hooks and sat up. I reached down and grabbed my water bottle that was next to me and took a sip.

A hand landed on my shoulder and I yelled, whipping around, spilling water all over me and the workout bench. A set of wide, yet very familiar, blue eyes greeted me.

"Tamara?" I wiped the water from my face and then pulled out my earbuds. I swung one leg over the bench and then stood.

Was this a dream? It was a strange dream if it was. But the longer I stared at her the more realization dawned on me.

Tamara was indeed standing there. She was thinner, her skin paler, and her eyes looked tired. Her clothes were baggy on her, hanging limply off her shoulders, but I could tell that they were clean. She looked like she'd been put through the wringer and come out the other side.

"What are you doing here?" I asked as I returned my earbuds to their case before giving her my undivided attention. The sense of relief that she was okay, contrasted against all of the questions that were racing through my mind.

"I—um..." She closed her eyes as she pressed her fore-fingers to her temples. "I'm..." She squeezed her eyes like what she was about to say was painful for her.

Hating that she was struggling, I closed the space between us and wrapped my arm around her shoulders. "It's okay," I whispered. I wasn't sure what was going on, but it hurt me to see someone I'd cared about like this.

Her body slumped against me as I guided her toward the back door of the inn. Once we were inside the kitchen, I sat her down next to the table and then stood. "I'll make us some coffee."

Thankfully, I'd just done a load of laundry yesterday, so I was able to locate a shirt in the dryer. Then I filled the coffee maker with water and turned it on, the hum of the machine filling the silence in the kitchen.

I grabbed a glass of ice water and moved to sit next to Tamara at the table. I set the baby monitor down next to me and then turned to studied Tamara. Her shoulders rounded and she was staring off into the distance. Her lips were pulled tight and her eyes looked tired.

She'd been a force to be reckoned with when I first met her. A whirlwind of laughter and joy, filling my boring world. It was strange to see the shell of a woman she'd become. She just looked worn out now. The light in her eyes that had distracted me for months had faded.

"You okay?" I finally asked, breaking the deafening silence between us.

She startled, whipping her gaze over to meet mine. "Hmm?" she asked.

I gave her a weak smile. "Are you okay?"

She studied me for a moment before tears began to fill her eyes. Her shoulders sagged even more as she tipped her gaze up to the ceiling, biting her lip and shaking her head. "No, Miles. I'm not."

A tear slipped down her cheek, and I reached for a napkin on the table and handed it to her. She took it and dabbed her eyes.

"What happened?"

She let out a small sigh before she glanced back up at me. "Phil died."

I blinked. "Who?"

"My boyfriend, Phil."

"He died?" Never in the few months we were together or when she'd dropped off Belle, had she mentioned a Phil. It was strange that she came all the way to Harmony just to tell me this. Especially since I didn't know him.

"Six months ago, he overdosed." She swallowed and then tipped her gaze up to the ceiling again. She tapped her fingers on the table a few times before turning her attention back to me. "That was rock bottom for me. I've been trying to get my life together ever since then." She closed her eyes for a moment. "My counselor told me the best thing to do is to return to a place where I felt safe."

I studied her. Here? The last place she felt safe was with me? Her gaze met mine, and that was all I needed to answer my questions. She needed me. She needed Harmony. If she was going to get better, she needed to be here to do that.

"Of course, Tamara. I'm happy to help." After all, how could I turn away the mother of my child? Especially when she looked so sad. So broken.

A smile played on her lips as the familiar twinkle in her eyes returned. "That makes me so happy. I was worried—"

Movement in the hallway drew our attention. My stomach dropped when I saw who was standing there. Shelby's eyes were wide as she glanced between Tamara and me. I cleared my throat and hurried to stand, not sure how I was going to explain what was going on and praying that she didn't misinterpret Tamara's sudden appearance.

"You're up," I blurted out as I started to cross the room. Then I kicked myself for descending on her so quickly. I stopped halfway between them. My focus was on Shelby, whose eyes were wide as she kept her gaze locked on Tamara, who was, consequently, now staring at me.

"Who's this?" Tamara asked.

I swallowed, all the muscles in my body tensing as I glanced between the two of them. There was no easing anyone into what was about to happen. There had been a few too many drunken nights when I'd stupidly confessed my broken heart to Tamara. She was very aware of what Shelby's return would mean to me.

I studied Shelby, hoping she would read my gaze and not freak out. I extended my hand toward Tamara and said, "Shelby, this is Tamara. Belle's mom."

Whatever Shelby had been expecting me to say, that was not it. Her eyes widened, and her jaw muscles flinched as she stared at me and then back to Tamara.

Tamara was studying me, and I knew the reason why. Her gaze screamed, *Shelby?* I wanted a hole to open up and swallow me as I stood there, watching the woman I loved and the mother of my daughter stare at each other.

"You're Belle's mom?" Shelby asked, extending her hand in the direction of Belle's room.

Tamara nodded. They shook hands for a moment before both women stepped back. "And you're Shelby. *The* Shelby."

Shelby looked confused as she glanced over at me and then back to Tamara. "You know who I am?" She closed her eyes and shook her head. "Of course you do. Did you know my grandmother? I mean, you were the librarian here. You had to have heard about her." Her words were picking up speed, and her voice was slowly rising an octave. She was overwhelmed. It took all of my strength not to ask Tamara to leave so I could calm Shelby down.

"Hey," I whispered as I closed the space between us and wrapped my arms around her. We'd had such a magical night last night, I didn't want her to forget that. I was here for her. I was always going to be here for her.

But Shelby didn't melt into my embrace like I'd expected her to. Instead, she just stood there like a rigid board. My heart ached. I'd finally coaxed her out of her shell, the last thing I wanted was for her to climb back in and fortify it to the point that I could never penetrate it again.

Worried that I'd overstepped, I dropped my arms and stepped back. I couldn't read Shelby's gaze as she stood there, frozen to the spot.

I needed to get Tamara settled somewhere else so I could talk to Shelby. I was trying to contain a fire, and in a few minutes, Belle was going to be up requiring the bulk of my attention. Plus, I wasn't ready to face how I felt about Tamara meeting Belle. Right now, I needed to focus on Shelby and my daughter. I'd worry about what Tamara's return meant later.

"Let me get you a key to a room and you can get settled," I said as I wrapped my hands around Tamara's shoulders and guided her through the swinging door and out to the dining room. Just as the door swung shut, I peeked back at Shelby. Thankfully, she didn't instantly take off. She stood there with her arms wrapped around her chest, staring down at the floor. My heart ached for her as I followed behind Tamara. Shelby was most likely in shock—and I'd brought that on her.

Pushing those thoughts from my mind for now, I grabbed a key from behind the desk and shoved it into Tamara's hand. She stared down at it while I told her how to find her room and promised I would come get her later so we could talk. I could see that she had questions, but I wasn't ready to answer any of them.

Thankfully, she had enough of her wits about her to nod and head up the stairs toward her room. Now alone, I sprinted back to the kitchen to find that Shelby had stayed right where I'd left her.

Not wanting to lose her again, I crossed the space between us and wrapped my arms around her, burying my face into her neck. "I'm so sorry. I didn't mean for you to meet her like that," I whispered as I pulled back.

Shelby glanced up at me, and I inwardly cursed when I couldn't read her gaze.

"How long has she been here?"

"Just this morning. She found me while I was working out." I gave her a weak smile, hoping she could see that Tamara meant nothing to me. That Tamara being back here hadn't changed my feelings for her.

Shelby studied me as if she were searching for sincerity in my gaze. It broke my heart. I wanted to be a safe place for her to land, and I hated that my history was as tangled as it was.

"Why is she back here?"

I reached out and brushed her fingers with mine. I waited for a moment to see if she would take my hand, and my heart sang when she spread her fingers and let mine in. Her skin was soft and cold against mine. I stepped closer, staring down at her with all the emotions that were coursing through me. Out of all the ways I'd imagined this morning going, this was not one I'd even thought possible.

"She needs some help right now. And as she's Belle's mom, I can't turn her away." I leaned in, my voice deepening with emotion. "But we are not getting back together. I meant what I said last night." I reached up and tucked her hair behind her ear, letting my fingers run from her hair down her neck, and I finished it off with a kiss to her clavicle.

She let out a soft sigh and tipped her head back, beckoning me in. My hand found her waist, and I pulled her against me. I trailed kisses from her neck to her lips. She let go of my fingers and slid her hands from my chest to my neck where she tightened her grip to deepen the kiss.

All the worry that had plagued my gut dissipated as I held her against my body. I wanted her to know that I was here for her. I was always going to be here for her. I broke our kiss to lean forward and whisper, "I love you," in her ear.

She pulled back and held my gaze. I could see the worry inside of her, and I wanted to put that fear to rest, once and for all.

"I mean it." My hand found her fingers, and I brought her knuckles to my lips and pressed a kiss into them, reveling in the fact that, this time, she was awake and watching me.

I could see her study me from over her hand, so I brought my gaze up to meet hers. She looked less panicked, but I could tell that she was still worried. I knew it was going to take her some time, but I could live with her worry.

What I couldn't live with was her leaving. And with our history, leaving was what I'd come to expect when it came to Shelby. So even though I was terrified that she was going to walk out on me once more, I was going to take her staying in this kitchen, kissing me, as a positive sign.

And those three little words that she still hadn't said to me? Well, her standing here in front of me, letting me touch her like I was, they were as good as spoken. It was only a matter of time before I heard those words come from her sexy lips. And I wasn't going anywhere until she felt safe enough to utter them.

I was willing to spend every moment of every day proving that to her.

I was never going to leave.

Ever.

2

SHELBY

SWEET TEA &
SOUTHERN GENTLEMAN

I FELT CONFUSED AND WORRIED, but the way Miles was holding me helped silence those fears...until he let me go. Belle was up, so he gave me one last parting kiss before he headed down the hallway and disappeared.

I told him that I would get started on breakfast, so I made my way to the fridge and stood in front of the open doors as I stared inside. With the way I was feeling, the only thing I could think to make was some eggs, bacon, and waffles. Simple. I grabbed the egg carton and milk before slamming the fridge door behind me.

Tamara was here.

I paused as I set the items down on the counter and closed my eyes. Of all the ways I'd imagined this morning going, seeing Belle's mom standing in the kitchen looking at Miles for an explanation as to why *I* was here, wasn't even close to what I'd pictured. I'd wanted it to be just

Miles and me until Belle woke up, and then it would be the three of us. We'd spend the day together, taking care of the inn, playing with Belle, and acting like...a family.

I had been such a fool to think that was even possible. Happiness wasn't in the cards for me. I knew that, but apparently, I was foolish enough to believe things could change.

I rested my hands on the counter and stepped back, allowing my head to fall forward as I closed my eyes. I took in a deep breath, stretching the muscles in my chest, then I blew out my breath. I fought the urge to sprint from the kitchen, pack up my things, and head back to New York. I had no job or boyfriend there, but at least my heart wouldn't be in danger of shattering like it could here.

"Excuse me." A soft voice startled me.

My entire body went numb when I turned to face the voice that I'd first heard earlier that morning. Once again, I was staring into the bright blue eyes of Tamara. She looked refreshed. Her hair was damp and her clothes were clean, albeit baggy.

She raised her hand as she stepped closer to me. "I'm sorry, I didn't mean to startle you, but I am in desperate need of some coffee, and the pot out there hasn't been filled yet." She motioned toward the dining room before offering me an apologetic smile.

She looked genuine, and I hated it. I needed to hate this woman. After all, she'd left Miles and Belle. Miles had told me why, and I did feel compassion for her, but it was no excuse. In the short amount of time I'd been back, I'd fallen hard for both Miles and Belle. How could she live with the fact that she'd walked away?

And how could she come back? What did she think would happen now that she was here? I narrowed my eyes, hardening my heart against the woman standing in front of me. If she thought she was going to become a part of my life, she had another thing coming.

"I bring out the pot and fill the dispenser in a minute," I said, my tone curt. I could hear my grandmother *tsk* at me for my reaction to Tamara, but I didn't care. I was going to act this way to anyone who hurt Miles and Belle, on purpose or not.

Her eyes widened—my tone hadn't been lost on her. "I—er..."

I folded my arms and stared at her, waiting for her to respond. I wasn't sure what she wanted from me, but a girl chat wasn't what she'd be getting. My emotions were a wreck. They'd been that way since I came back to Harmony. And just when I thought I was finding happiness once more, she had to come back and rip that rug out from under my feet.

"Miles told you about me." Her voice was a whisper now.

I glanced over my shoulder and saw that she had no intention of leaving. Instead, she'd moved to lean against the counter behind her and tip her head back. I took in a deep breath, wishing she would just go. I wasn't ready for this conversation. I didn't want to get to know her, and I feared the longer she talked to me, the harder it would be to keep my walls up.

"He honestly didn't say much. Just that you showed up on his doorstep and left him with Belle." I glanced over at her once more to see her studying me. "I filled in the rest. I turned to the cupboard and pulled out the waffle machine then plugged it in so it could warm up.

"I was wrong," she whispered, so quiet that I almost didn't hear her.

I stopped angrily moving things around so I could make out her words. "You were wrong?"

She nodded. Even from where I was standing, I could see tears filling her eyes. "I should have never left like that. I shouldn't have abandoned Belle. She just wasn't..." Her voice broke as she wiped away the tear that fell. She pinched her lips together and stared hard at a spot in front of her. Then she took in a deep breath. "I should have never left Miles. He's such a good guy. I knew he would take care of her, and I..." Her voice trailed off.

I wasn't sure why she was telling me these things. Was she hoping that I would help her get Miles to talk to her? That he would listen and they would get back together again? My stomach was knotted so tight that I couldn't breathe. All I wanted to do was vomit.

"Well, what you did was crappy." The words passed my lips before I could stop them. My eyes widened as I glanced over at her. She looked startled but not surprised.

I continued, "My mom left me in a similar fashion, and it wasn't fun." It wasn't until the words were out that I realized my reaction to her had more layers that I cared to admit. And I hated discovering this in her presence as she stared at me.

I felt vulnerable and raw, and I all wanted to do was run away. Run far away from Harmony Inn, Tamara, and whatever was going to happen between me and Miles. But I couldn't do that. At least, not right now. Not when Miles seemed to have his head in the clouds, thinking that we could just carry on like we had yesterday.

The truth was, things had changed. And it was only a matter of time until Miles came to that same conclusion.

"I'm sorry," Tamara whispered as she pressed her fingers into her palms.

An awkward silence fell over us, so I whisked up the waffle batter as the iron beeped that it was ready. I was done with this conversation, and I prayed that she would leave me alone.

"I'm happy you're back."

I stopped whisking and turned to her. "What?"

She offered me a weak smile. "I heard a lot about you while I lived here. And when Miles brought me to meet Charlotte, she did nothing else but talk about you."

I stared at her. At the mention of my grandmother my entire body stiffened. How dare this stranger say these things to me? How dare she act like she knew me because she was part of the gossip train that ran rampant here in

Harmony? She didn't know my grandmother. And what she was saying was a lie.

A hurtful lie that ripped at the fraying threads holding my heart together.

My grandmother hadn't talked about me. Our relationship was over the moment I drove away. And imagining something different was affecting me in a way that I wasn't ready to face.

And I certainly didn't want to sit here and discuss it with a stranger. Desperate for something to do, I picked up the mixing bowl and continued whisking, my body taking over so my mind could sort through its confusion.

"Tamara." Miles' voice jolted me. I turned to see him walking into the kitchen with Belle resting on his arm. He hurried over to the high chair and set her inside. "What are you doing here? I thought I told you I'd come get you later."

Tamara's eyes widened as her gaze drifted from Miles to Belle. Our conversation didn't seem to have the same effect on her as it had on me. In fact, from the way she kept looking from Belle to Miles, our conversation was very much forgotten. Which only angered me more. Here I was, feeling as if my heart were ripped out and bleeding on the floor while Tamara looked unfazed by it all. Her cheeks were flushed and her body still as her focus was fixed on Belle.

I was left with unwanted memories and thoughts of

my grandmother mixed with the ache that came from watching the reunion of this little family.

Miles met my gaze for a moment before he crossed the room and stared down at Tamara. "Please, just wait for me in the dining room." His hand went to her elbow.

Jealousy pricked at my gut, so I turned back to the waffle iron and began to pour the batter in. Tamara responded with a whisper, but it was too quiet for me to hear and I wasn't in the mood to try to listen in.

I blinked a few times, hating that Miles and Tamara had a history together. That they could speak to each other in hushed tones. She had an intimacy with Miles that I was never going to have. They were parents to Belle, and that was a role I was never going to be able to fill. I would never be Belle's mom, no matter how much I wished I could.

The smell of baking waffles filled the air, and any other day, it would calm me. But today they just made my stomach churn. From the corner of my eye, I could see Tamara nod and disappear through the swinging door. Now alone, Miles stood rooted to the spot like he was trying to decide what to do.

"I'm not feeling too good," I whispered as I stepped back from the counter. "I got the batter mixed, and there's a waffle cooking." I moved closer to the back door just as Miles turned to study me. "I'm going to go to my cottage, if that's okay." Right now, that seemed to be the only safe place for me.

I needed to cry. I needed to nurse my hangover. And I needed to come up with a game plan. I couldn't do those things with Miles staring at me the way he was. Or touching me the way he had this morning.

"Shelby..." Miles' whisper caused my entire body to ache. It amazed me that so much could be said with a single uttered word. I waited to hear what he was going to say. Instead, he closed his lips and nodded. "I'll handle breakfast. You go take some time."

He wanted to say more. I could see it in the way his jaw muscles strained and the way his gaze felt as if it was going to bore a hole through me. I could see fear in the back of his gaze. He was worried I was going to leave like I had before.

Even though that thought had crossed my mind, there was no way I could leave. At least, not right now. I just needed some time and space to figure out what I was going to do.

"I'll come by this afternoon," I whispered.

His eyes lit up. "Really?"

I nodded as my fingers played with the door handle behind me. "I'm not leaving town if that's what you're worried about."

He furrowed his brow. I could see that he wanted to deny it, but he just sighed and gave me a smile. "Thanks."

I pursed my lips and nodded. Then I turned the handle and pulled open the door. He didn't call out for me to stay as I stepped onto the porch and shut the door behind me. Once I was out from under the intensity of his gaze, I hurried across the yard and pulled open the cottage door.

I didn't hesitate once I was safely inside. I stripped off the clothes he'd let me borrow, folded them, and buried them deep in my closet. I wasn't ready to give them back. But I also didn't want them out where I could see them. They would remain in the depths of my closet until I was strong enough to do something with them.

I headed into the bathroom and turned on the shower. Steam filled the room, and I was instantly brought back to last night, standing in the bathroom with Miles. I closed my eyes and pictured the way he stared at me like I was the only thing in this life he wanted.

I felt desire in the way he touched and kissed me.

My heart began to race as the desire I had for him raged in my stomach. I wanted all of him. Emotionally, mentally...physically.

I squeezed my eyes shut, tipped my head back, and cursed the heavens. I hated that I had let my guard down. I should have known that fate was only going to rip away any semblance of happiness for me. I was destined to remain alone and heartbroken forever.

I stepped into the shower and let the water beat against my back. I closed my eyes as the tears fell. I knew it was going to wreak havoc on my hangover, but I didn't care. I needed to let these tears out.

Deep down, I feared that everything had changed.

Tamara was back. Those three words pierced every corner of my mind. Even if Miles pretended that it didn't matter, I knew it did.

Regardless of how I felt about Miles, I loved Belle. She was not only the sweetest thing to bless my life, but in a strange, stupid way, she represented me. And if I could give her a different future than the one I'd been saddled with, I was going to do that. I had to.

I felt better when I flipped off the shower and stepped out. I dried off with a towel before wrapping it around my body and another one around my hair.

I padded out to my kitchen. My head ached from the humidity of the shower mixed with crying, and I knew the only cure for that was some coffee. I stopped dead in my tracks. Miles' back was to me as if he were trying to slip out.

"Miles?"

He stopped, his shoulders tightening before he turned around, a sheepish expression filled his face. "Sorry."

Heat pricked my skin as I watched his gaze drop to my towel. I wrapped my arms around the top for security. I needed to keep my wits about me, even though every molecule in my body wanted me to walk over and let him touch every part of me.

When his gaze returned to mine, my breath caught in my throat. He was thinking the same thing.

"What are you doing here?" I asked, clearing my throat and forcing myself to remain calm.

He pushed his hand through the front part of his hair but paused, resting his head in his hand. I hated that I could see the muscles in his upper arm. Or the small tattoo that I'd never noticed before. It looked like the rose from *Beauty and the Beast*.

Thankfully, his gaze was focused on the window overlooking the small flower garden next to the cottage and not on me as I stared at his tattoo. The last thing I needed was for him to think that I was interested in any part of his body. I needed to keep my distance if I was going to keep my sanity.

He blew out his breath and finished pushing his hand through his hair as his gaze dropped back to me. "I was just worried, that's all."

I shook my head as I padded over to the fridge and opened it. "I said I wasn't going to go anywhere, and I'm a woman of my word." I bent over to grab a water bottle and then turned, shutting the fridge door with my foot.

Miles' gaze was fixed on my legs, and I waited for him to realize that I was watching him. When his gaze finally returned to mine, he offered me a sheepish smile. "Sorry."

I shrugged as I cracked the cap. "We should probably put all of that on hold," I said as I held the bottle to my lips. Once I was finished speaking, I tipped the bottom of the water bottle up, letting the cool liquid coat my throat.

I watched him from over the bottle. His gaze went from one of distraction to one of focus.

"What?" he asked.

I slowly lowered the bottle before twisting the top back on. "I think we need to put this"—I waved between our bodies—"on hold."

He furrowed his brow. "On hold?"

I nodded, hating that my throat crackled every time I swallowed. Tears pricked my eyes as my heart pounded its resistance to the words that lingered on the tip of my tongue. "We can't pursue this, you and I." My voice was hoarse.

Miles closed the space between us as if my words had finally registered. "Shelby, no." I took a step back, bumping into the counter behind me, but he didn't let up on his advance. His arms surrounded my body as he rested his hands behind me, caging me in. "Please, I don't want to be with Tamara."

Tears stung my eyes. I blinked a few times hoping to push them back, but they flowed down my cheeks. All of my senses were going haywire from his proximity and the way he was staring into my eyes, and the resolve that I'd come to while in the shower was faltering.

"I just don't think you can say that right now," I whispered.

Miles frowned, his gaze never leaving mine. "What do you mean?"

I closed my eyes for a moment as I gathered my strength. I offered him a weak smile, hoping it would help calm him down. "Tamara's back, and if you can make things work with her, you should."

Those words felt like a knife to my chest. I straightened, hoping he would take the hint and back away. But he didn't move. Instead, he continued to watch me. "Why are you saying this?"

I swallowed and wiped my tears from my cheeks. "Because it's what Belle deserves. She deserves to have her parents try to make it work."

Miles' frown deepened for a moment before he glanced to the side and cursed under his breath. "Don't say that."

"It's true."

He pushed away from me and moved to lean against the counter on the other side of the kitchen. His shoulders were rounded as he stared at the ground. I could feel the turmoil going on inside of him.

It matched my own.

"Let's just give *us* some space. We need time to figure out what we want." I was babbling now, but I was trying to keep my heart from breaking.

He didn't move. He continued to stare at the ground. I wrapped my arms around my chest as I took in a deep breath. I knew when he walked out the door, everything was going to change.

I wanted him to stay, but I also wanted him to go. I wanted him to agree with me and walk away. It would pulverize my heart, but it would make leaving at the end of the six months easier.

I was weak when he asked me to stay. I was weak

when he begged to me not to leave him. Every ounce of self-control that I thought I had went out the window when it came to Miles. I knew where my limits were, but I wasn't prepared to uphold those limits when he was around.

I wasn't prepared for the push and pull.

"Is that what you want?" he finally asked as he brought his gaze up to mine.

The pain I saw there took my breath away. I wanted to say no. I wanted him to beg me to stay. But I couldn't do that to him. So I just nodded. "Yes."

He remained quiet as he stared at me. Then he pushed off the counter and nodded. "Okay."

He brought his hand up to rub his neck and then rolled his shoulders. "If that's what you want, then I'll play along." He took a few steps toward me, and my body shuddered in anticipation. But he never touched me. "Just promise me one thing."

I slowly brought my gaze up to meet his before I nodded. "Okay," I whispered.

"Promise me that you'll stay here. And that if you leave..." His voice broke, causing tears to once again prick my eyelids. "You'll tell me."

I stared at him, drinking in his familiar blue eyes and the look of affection that had swept me away yesterday. Scared that I would beg him to love me forever if I opened my mouth, I just nodded.

That seemed to appease him. He stared at me for a

moment longer before he stepped around me and left. The sound of the front door closing filled the silent air.

I let out a sob as I sunk to the floor. I wrapped my arms around my waist, and my heart felt as if it were breaking. I hadn't wanted any of this, but it was the hand I was dealt.

At some point, things would feel better. But for now, I was going to sit on the kitchen floor in my towel and cry.

It felt like the only thing I could do.

3

ABIGAIL

SWEET TEA &
SOUTHERN GENTLEMAN

THE SOLID KNOCK on my door startled me. I sat up straight in my bed, and after a quick look at the clock on my nightstand, I groaned.

I'd slept in.

I pulled the covers from my body and swung my feet to the floor. The knock sounded again, so I grabbed my robe as I hurried to my bedroom door and pulled it open. Sabrina's eyes were bloodshot as she held out Samuel, who was screaming. His little face was bright red, his eyes were closed, and his mouth was open wider than I'd ever seen before.

"Sabrina." I exhaled as she dropped him into my arms.

"He won't stop screaming. I'm exhausted. You need to take over," she mumbled as she pushed her greasy hair behind her ear and turned. She didn't bother to meet my gaze. Instead, she disappeared into her room, shutting the door behind her.

I stared after her both shocked and annoyed. Sleep was still clinging to the folds of my brain. I needed coffee and a hot shower if I was going to feel human.

But from the way Samuel was arching his back and wailing, he wasn't going to let me do either.

Luckily, auntie mode kicked in. I brought him up to my shoulder and patted his back with my free hand as I started to bounce him. I shushed him as I walked down the hallway to the kitchen.

"Just let me get some coffee," I murmured as I pulled the dirty coffee pot out of the sink and sighed.

Sabrina had done very little yesterday in the way of cleaning the apartment, and I'd been too exhausted—and confused—to muster any strength of my own. Now, I was cursing myself for not taking care of the essentials while Samuel was passed out last night.

Samuel's crying wasn't letting up, and my head was pounding. I grabbed everything I needed to make a bottle, hoping that he was just hungry. I stood in the middle of the kitchen with my finger on the nipple of the bottle, shaking the powdered milk, as Samuel screamed in my ear.

I had so much to process from yesterday. Anders. His behavior toward me. Bash...

But my mind wasn't even willing to attempt to put any thoughts together with Samuel screaming like he was.

With the milk thoroughly mixed, I made my way

toward the living room. Just as I passed by the front door, I heard a knock. I stopped and glanced over, wondering if I was hearing things. I took another step forward only to hear the knock once more.

A shiver raced down my spine as I turned to face the door. I glanced at the clock. It was 6:30 in the morning. Who was here this early?

I peeked through the peep hole, but I didn't see anyone. Samuel's yowling had settled down to a faint whimper which helped my sleepy mind focus. I knew I'd heard something, even if no one was currently standing in the hallway. Feeling brave, I grabbed the door handle and peeked out. There was no one there. I shook my head and turned, only to spot something on the ground.

It was a cup of coffee set next to a brown paper bag. I stared at it for a moment then glanced around to see if the gifter was lingering at the far end of the hallway. But the quiet morning air was all that greeted me. I frowned as I peered further out. The jostling must have upset Samuel because he released another scream.

I hurried to collect the coffee and bag and slipped back into the apartment, shutting the door behind me. I set the bag down on the kitchen counter, but took the coffee with me while I pinched Samuel's bottle between my chin and chest and headed into the living room to find a chair.

The coffee could be laced with something, but I didn't care. I needed a pick-me-up if I was going to get through the morning. And with Samuel only seeming to relax in my arms, I knew there was no way I was going to have an stolen moment of time for self-care. Once I settled down on the rocking chair, Samuel happily took the bottle, and I rested my head back and closed my eyes, using my big toe to rock the chair.

My mind drifted back to Bash and what had happened yesterday. He'd been helping me with the dishes, but when the plate broke he suddenly went into panic mode.

Did he have PTSD? Was he ex-military? Was he a spy?

I shook my head. Anders didn't seem to be spy material, so where would he and Bash have met? Plus, from the way Bash cradled that chipmunk in his hands, he didn't seem like the kind of person who would hurt a fly.

I sighed, shifting my arm so I could grab the coffee and take a drink. Realizing that the coffee was probably for Sabrina—she did have a habit of ordering food deliveries— I guiltily glanced in the direction of her room.

Something was up with my sister. I wasn't sure what it was, but I was beginning to get concerned. Something needed to change. I feared what could happen while I was at work. Her behavior was moving quickly from tired, exhausted mom to something more dangerous.

But that was the problem with living in a small town. If I took her to see Dr. Thornton, the news would be all over the place, and that was the last thing Sabrina needed. Harmony's gossip train had been known to drive women in this town insane. If my sister was struggling, a bunch of women talking behind her back wasn't going to help.

I glanced down at my nephew and smiled. I loved the kid. His eyes were already slits even though only half of his bottle was gone. He must have cried for a while before Sabrina came and got me. He was exhausted. His little tongue had slipped off the nipple, but he was still sucking like it was there. I tried to move it around in his mouth to get him to wake up, but he was out. A slow trail of milk dripped from the corner of his mouth.

I set the bottle down, wiped his lips, and swaddled him before setting him in the bassinet.

With him taken care of, I finished off the coffee, vowing to order Sabrina some more when I got to work. I brushed off my guilt by telling myself that by the time she got up, it would have been cold, anyways. So I was, in fact, helping her.

I left the blueberry scone on the counter as a peace offering before I hurried into the bathroom to shower. Once I was clean and dressed, I slipped on my shoes, grabbed my purse and phone, then hurried from my room.

I knocked on Sabrina's door, but when she didn't answer, I pushed into the room to find her blinds were drawn shut and she was tangled up in a lump of pillows and blankets on the bed. I shook her shoulder a few times, and when I received an annoyed grunt, I let her know that I was leaving.

She just mumbled and snuggled deeper into the

covers. I moved to the door, taking one last look at her before I headed out into the hallway. Hopefully when Samuel woke up, she would hear his cries.

I made my way through the front door and down the back steps. Once I got to my car, I started it up and headed into town, praying that everyone else was running as behind as I was.

No such luck. I pulled up in front of the bookstore just as a line of construction workers began to form. I sighed as I grabbed my purse and hurried across the sidewalk.

"Sorry, guys," I said, pushing my damp hair from my face and offering them a smile. "Crazy morning."

They all murmured, "It's okay," or "That's fine," from behind me. I offered to let them in even though nothing was ready, and they gratefully accepted my offer. My heart sang as they wandered over to the books and began perusing them.

My mind went on autopilot as I started getting things ready for breakfast. Luckily, I'd baked a ton of pumpkin muffins yesterday so my glass case looked full. I also had some sugar cookies and maple sugar scones to offer.

With my coffee pot brewing, I slipped on my apron and gave the men a wide smile.

They didn't linger long once they picked up their orders. I was grateful that one decided to purchase a kid's book, stating it was for his niece back home. They all said their thank you's as they pushed through the door and headed back outside.

Now alone, I rested my elbows on the countertop and let my focus soften as my mind relaxed. I had a few minutes before I was going to force myself to get back to work. I had regulars coming in, and they were going to be disappointed if I didn't have their drinks ready.

But I couldn't help but think back to Bash and what happened yesterday. Perhaps it was the fact that Anders was out of town, or the fact that every time I looked at the sink, I thought about what happened yesterday, but I wanted to know more about him.

Was that bad?

I shook my head as I straightened, pushing away from the counter. Of course that was bad. What was wrong with me?

"Lack of sleep," I murmured as I grabbed the washcloth that I'd pulled out of the drawer and held it under the water.

And that was partly true. I was exhausted. Work mixed with Samuel had me feeling like I was a zombie.

The ding from the door made me look up. Willow Gentlesman walked in, her hair blown from the wind outside. She was pulling Jasper, her five-year-old son, behind her. She had an apron tied around her waist and an exasperated look in her eye. I didn't know her super well. She'd moved to town a few weeks back. Her great-uncle Douglas ran Harmony Island Diner, but he was sick and there were rumors that he was close to passing.

I gave her a smile to which she just exhaled.

"I'm so sorry to ask, but do you have a bathroom we can use?"

I set down the washcloth and nodded as I rounded the corner. "Of course. Just back there, first door on the left."

Willow gave me a thankful smile as she hurried in the direction I'd motioned. "I told him to go before we left," she said over her shoulder as she began to close the door.

"It's fine," I said, but the door was already shut.

Now alone, I grabbed the dishrag and wiped down the counters as I mentally prepped myself to make some lemon poppyseed muffins. I really wasn't in the mood to bake, which was strange for me. Making delicious morsels had always been a distraction from my life in the past. But now that I had to do it for money—the joy was starting to faulter.

Movement by the large picture window in the front of the shop drew my attention over. It looked like a jacket flapping in the wind, as if there was someone standing just beyond my sight. I thought at first someone was just leaning on the outside of the building, but looking closer, it seemed as if they were facing the shop.

Facing me.

I set my towel down on the counter and headed over to the door. Just as I pushed it open, I saw the person slip around the corner. Frustrated, I hurried to stop them.

"Hey," I said as I grabbed his elbow. "What are you —Bash?"

Bash's gaze was focused on the ground. He had a baseball cap pulled down over his face and wore a black shirt and dark jeans. He looked like a kid who had just been caught with his hand in the cookie jar.

"What are you doing out here?" I asked as I quickly dropped my hand and folded my arms across my chest.

Bash's entire body was stiff as he continued to stare at the gravel at his feet. Eventually, he peeked up at me only to drop his gaze once more. "I'm sorry."

I frowned. "For what?"

He exhaled. "Making you stop what you were doing. I was just checking to make sure..." His voice trailed off.

I studied him. "Make sure what?"

He rolled his shoulders and then shrugged, bringing his gaze up to meet mine. He rubbed the back of his neck. "Just making sure you were okay."

I stared at him. "Am I not okay?"

"Oh, that's not what I meant." He raised his hands in front of him. "I just promised Anders that I would look in on you, that's all."

The sound of the door opening drew my attention over. Willow was pulling Jasper from the store. Her expression faltered when she saw Bash, but she didn't waste any time asking who he was. The town had been filling up with construction workers, so we were becoming accustomed to new faces.

"Thanks so much," she said as she headed down the sidewalk.

"Anytime." But she was already halfway down the

block, so I doubted she even heard me. I turned my attention to Bash only to find him watching me once more.

He was so strange, and I couldn't figure him out. He didn't break my gaze as we just stared at each other. Finally, I sighed and motioned toward the shop. "Why don't you come in for some coffee." He parted his lips, and I could see his protest, so I grabbed his elbow. He stiffened, but that didn't stop me. "I'm not taking no for an answer. You're coming in."

He let me push him into the shop and over to the counter. I commanded that he sit, and he did. I rounded the counter and made my way over to the coffee pot and brought it up to show him. "Coffee?"

He shook his head. "No, thanks. I've already had some today."

I grabbed out a mug and filled it for myself. "Me too, but I'm exhausted." I sighed as I stirred in some creamer and sugar. Once the black liquid had turned milky, I took a sip and closed my eyes, letting out a soft moan. "I needed this." Realizing that I was having a moment with my coffee in front of Bash, my cheeks heated. I glanced over at him and shrugged. "I like coffee."

His gaze was dark and hard to read, but I could see a soft half smile emerge for a moment before it disappeared. "I know."

I quirked an eyebrow. "You do?"

He paused before his cheeks flushed, making me

giggle. "I mean, I figured. You turned your bookstore into a coffee shop. So I put two and two together."

I glanced around my shop and nodded. "Yeah. I guess it wouldn't take a detective to figure this out."

He smiled, but this time it felt forced. "Nope. It wouldn't take a detective."

I eyed him as I took another sip of my coffee. Why was this man so hard to read? How did he and Anders meet? Why was he here in my shop so early in the morning?

I narrowed my eyes, which only made him widen his own.

"What?" he asked.

I just continued to stare at him. There was something going on, but I couldn't quite put my finger on it. I let him suffer under my gaze for a moment longer before I set my mug down and turned toward the pastry case. "Muffin?"

"No, I'm actually quite—"

"I make the best muffins in all of Harmony. Just ask the ribbons I've won." I nodded toward the bright blue Harmony Island Festival first place ribbon I'd stuck to the bulletin board behind me. I set a pumpkin muffin down in front of Bash before stepping back. "It really is a town treasure."

Bash was watching me from behind his dark lashes. I held his gaze, daring him to turn me down. And to my surprise, he didn't. He grabbed the muffin and pulled the wrapper down before taking a large bite. I watched him closely, trying to gauge his reaction. For some reason, I wanted him to like the muffin.

And that frustrated me.

He nodded and took another bite. I took that as a good sign and moved to pull out the ingredients for the lemon poppyseed muffins I needed to make. "You can report that back to your superior," I said as I began to dump flour into the mixing bowl.

I laughed softly at my own joke, but when I looked up at Bash, he just looked startled. I furrowed my brow as he continued to stare at me.

"Your superior," I said again, frustrated that I had to explain my joke.

"Superior?"

I held his gaze. "Yeah. Anders?"

He paused and then laughed. It was loud and forced. I studied him before I turned my attention back to pouring sugar into the bowl. That was strange. But from what I knew of Bash—which was very little—everything about him seemed a tad strange.

My best friend in high school had a brother who didn't pick up on humor and often took jokes literally. Perhaps that was Bash.

When I looked back at him, he'd inhaled the rest of the muffin and was moving to stand. I watched him wipe the crumbs off the counter onto the muffin wrapper before he crumpled it up.

"Leaving so soon?"

He paused his chewing to look up. Then he nodded as he swallowed his food. "Yeah, I've got things to do."

I hooked the bowl to my mixer and threaded the paddle on. "Oh, okay." I gave him a small smile. "Thanks for stopping by." I flipped the mixer on and it hummed to life.

Bash's gaze turned serious for a moment before he nodded. "Of course." He pulled off his cap and pushed his hands through his hair before returning his cap. "I—er—"

"Next time," I started, hoping to lessen the awkwardness between us, "just come in. Don't make me come out and get you." I shrugged as I lifted my hands up. "It's just a bookstore-slash-coffee shop. Anyone can be in here. You don't need an invitation."

Bash glanced around the shop before returning his gaze to me. He studied me for a moment before he nodded. "Okay."

He didn't wait for me respond before he pushed through the front doors and disappeared around the building. I watched for a moment longer, just to see if he was going to return to his earlier post. But the front of the building seemed quiet, so I returned to making my muffins.

Fifteen minutes later, as I was slipping the muffins into the oven, the front door opened and Shelby rushed in. I shut the oven door and turned around to find her leaning on the counter, her hair disheveled and her eyes wild.

"Everything okay?" I asked as I set down my oven mitts and turned to give her my full attention.

"Coffee," she whispered as she slipped onto a bar stool.

I nodded and filled her a mug. Once I set it down in front of her, she took a sip and winced.

"It's hot," I said as I handed her some creamer.

She tapped her tongue with her fingertip and nodded. "I got that." She dumped in some creamer and then took another sip.

Once half the coffee was gone, she set the mug down on the counter. I raised my eyebrows when she met my gaze.

"Wanna tell me now?"

She covered her face with her hands and let out a breath before peeking through her fingers and whispering, "Tamara's back."

4

SHELBY

SWEET TEA & SOUTHERN GENTLEMAN

THE MOMENT that Abigail saw me, a look of concern passed over her face. I realized that I must look like the wreck that I felt inside. I'd managed to peel myself off the kitchen floor and get dressed. But I hadn't waited for my hair to dry or taken the time to put on makeup. I'd just grabbed my purse and climbed into the car.

My tires spun against the gravel as I sped away from Harmony Inn and drove straight to The Shop Around the Corner. The only place in this godforsaken town that felt safe.

And now, sitting here, seeing Abigail study me, the tears began to flow. I wanted to speak, but when I tried, sobs just slipped out.

Abigail seemed to know what to do. She pulled her lips into a tight line, slipped out from behind the counter, and locked the front door after she flipped the *open* sign to *closed.*

When she got back to the small kitchen, she poured me another mug of coffee and grabbed the largest chocolate chip cookie from her display case. I took it, nodding my thanks.

Half a cookie and all of my coffee later, I sniffled as I grabbed a nearby napkin and wiped my tears.

Abigail studied me, patiently waiting for me to explain. All I'd given her was, "Tamara's back," before the tears began to flow and words escaped my mind. Now that I felt better, I was ready to talk.

"She showed up this morning," I whispered as I continuously folded and unfolded the napkin I'd wiped my cheeks with.

"Tamara," Abigail repeated.

I nodded. "Tamara."

"Belle's mom."

I nodded again.

"Why did she come back?"

I shrugged. "She's trying to get her life together or something. I don't know." I blew out my breath as I tipped my face toward the ceiling. I closed my eyes for a moment before I returned my focus to Abigail.

"Did Miles..." Abigail started before she stopped. I could see the hesitation in her gaze.

I shook my head. "He told me that he doesn't want to be with her. He wants...me." The last word emerged as a whisper as I dropped my gaze to the napkin and tears once again filled my eyes. Why couldn't I get a grip on my emotions? I was turning into a mess.

Abigail reached out and covered my hand with hers. "If this doesn't change anything between you two, why are you so upset?"

I swallowed, emotions causing a lump to form in my throat. "Because I know how this is going to end," I said, offering a weak smile.

She frowned. "How is it going to end?"

My smile faded. "With the two of them together."

"But you just said that Miles doesn't want to be with her."

I nodded. "But I can't be with Miles if there is an opportunity for the two of them to work it out. Belle deserves everything that I never had." I sighed as I dropped my gaze down to the counter in front of me and began to pick up crumps. Then I dusted my fingers off over my plate. My stomach was in knots from my emotions and the cookie I'd inhaled faster than I cared to admit.

Abigail shifted her weight as she pressed her fingers to the bridge of her nose. "Shelby, I don't think—"

"Can I spend the afternoon here?" I asked, breaking off her words. I feared what she was going to say if I let her talk. The truth was, I couldn't face this situation anymore. I was broken, and I feared what the future held. Miles told me that he was always going to protect me, but I just didn't know how he was going to do that without breaking his vow to protect his daughter.

No matter how much he wanted reality to be different, no choice he could make was going to make us both happy. He was going to have to choose. And I knew, deep down, that if he chose me, I would never forgive him.

Pain coated my chest, making it hard to breath. Pain pressed on my mind, making it hard to form thoughts. I just needed some time, and I hoped I'd find it here. When I finally glanced up at Abigail, she was still watching me, but she must have understood what I needed because her expression had turned to one of understanding. "Sure, you can stay here as long as you need. Wanna help me out?"

I smiled. "That would be great."

She clapped her hands together before walking to the backroom and returning with an apron. "I do have to tell you, Missy hasn't made her morning visit yet. But if she comes, you can relax in the backroom until she leaves."

My stomach churned at the mention of Missy's name, but I was so distracted that those feelings quickly dissipated.

Abigail unlocked the shop and started me in the back washing the dishes. I was grateful for the distraction as I ran my hands under the warm water filling up the sink. She'd made some lemon poppyseed muffins, so I zeroed in on scrubbing the batter from her large mixing bowl.

It was monotonous and didn't take any brain power to do. And right now, that was all I needed.

After I finished the dishes, I wiped my hands on the drier part of the towel as I walked out from the back. Abigail was cleaning out the fridge, so I moved to join her. We worked in silence for a few minutes before Abigail's gaze made its way to me.

I could see she still had so many questions, and I wasn't ready to answer any of them.

"What are you plans for the shop?" I asked, hoping to distract her.

She paused, narrowing her eyes, but then started in on how her dad and stepmom were coming to Harmony from a small town in Rhode Island called Magnolia. She needed to dust the shelves to get ready for a signing she was hosting for an author named Jackson Richards.

Her eyes sparkled when she talked about the author. I loved that she had things to look forward to. It made me want the same.

"What about you?" she asked. And when I blinked and focused on her, I realized that she had just repeated herself.

I shrugged as I pulled out the bottle of buttermilk and checked the best by date. "Well, I'll be heading to New York next weekend."

Abigail stopped moving. The sourdough starter she'd just pulled out was perched on her open hand. "What?"

I shook my head. "Don't worry. I'm not leaving forever. I just have a commitment that I have to fulfill."

After Miles left this morning, I'd gotten a text from

Titan asking if we were still on. Relief flooded my body when I read it. Truth was, I'd kind of forgotten about our arrangement, and yesterday, I would have turned him down. Yesterday, I hadn't cared what would happen to my career in New York or my reputation. I'd wanted Harmony and Miles, and there hadn't been anything that was going to stop me.

But now I wasn't sure. I needed to keep my options open. And if that meant going to Titan's sister's wedding as his date, I was going to go. Even though Abigail and Miles seemed convinced that Tamara's return meant nothing had changed, I wasn't naive enough to think that my future was secure.

I needed a contingency plan in place.

Abigail didn't break her stare as she zeroed in on me. "Does Miles know that you are leaving?"

I shook my head as I pulled out a bag of fresh blueberries and set them on the counter. "I got the text from Titan right before I left to come here."

"Titan?"

I nodded as I stared into the fridge. Truth was, Abigail's stare was too much. I felt weak when she looked at me, and I hated it. To her, everything made sense. But I was so confused, and I hated that I didn't see things as black-and-white as she did.

"He's a...friend from New York that needs me to be his plus one at a wedding."

"Friend?"

This was a fun conversation. "Yep."

"Who needs you to be his date."

I nodded.

Suddenly, I felt Abigail's hand on my arm as I was leaning into the fridge to pull out a Tupperware container. "Shelby."

I paused, anxiety filling my gut about what she was going to say. Was I prepared to digest it? Was she going to try to convince me to stay? I wasn't ready to hear her argument if that was her goal. "Yeah?" I asked, dusting off my fear and turning to face her.

Her brows were drawn together, and her gaze was so focused that I felt like I was going to melt under her stare. "Why are you leaving?"

I shrugged, hating this interrogation. "I'm not leaving. I'm just fulfilling a commitment I made before I even came down here." Before I fell in love with Miles.

When Abigail didn't respond, I peeked over at her. Her arms were folded and her eyes narrowed as she watched me. She didn't believe me, but that was okay for now. I needed to do what was necessary to protect my heart.

She had to understand that.

"So where's your boy? Did he stop by this morning?" I leaned against the counter with my arms crossed. I wasn't the only one struggling in the male population department. And I was kind of tired of this one-sided conversation. I wanted to take the focus off of my lovelife.

Abigail's cheeks turned pink and she dropped her hands, turning to the fridge. "Anders is still out of town," she mumbled as she pulled out a pitcher of coffee creamer and set it on the counter.

"He is?" She wasn't meeting my gaze, and her cheeks were turning a deeper red by the second. It was a strange reaction. "Then why are you blushing like a schoolgirl?" I waved toward her face.

Her hands went to her cheeks as her eyes widened. "I'm not blushing."

I snorted. "Yes, you are. I'm so confused."

She shook her head. "Just thinking about Anders and what it'll be like when he gets back."

I narrowed my eyes. Things weren't adding up here. "Uh huh," I said, making sure to drag out the sound so she knew that I didn't believe her.

She shot me a smile over her shoulder as she clapped her hands together. "Let's get these shelves wiped down, make a list of what we need to replace, and load the fridge back up."

I wanted to ask more questions; Abigail was acting suspicious. But I was ready to get away from talking about our love lives and focus on something else. Abigail seemed to want the same thing.

She turned on some music, and we kept the conversation light as we cleaned. Then I grabbed a pad of paper and began to make a list of the items she shouted out so she could be heard over the music. Once the list was made, I turned to see a figure at the front door.

My entire heart stopped when I saw it was Missy. She had her sunglasses perched on the tip of her nose, her phone pressed to her cheek, and her purse dangling from her arm as she reached out for the handle.

I dropped to the floor with the pen and pad of paper still in hand. Abigail looked startled, but when I nodded toward the front door, understanding crossed her face. She waved me toward the back, and I slunk in the direction she motioned.

"Missy," she called out, a tad louder than normal.

I didn't wait to hear Missy's response. Instead, I pressed my back to the wall and shut the door. Now that I was safely hidden, I let out my breath, doubling over to calm my pounding heart.

I'd felt so good, laughing and working in the shop with Abigail, and I hated to have that ripped away from me at the sight of the woman who made my life miserable when I'd lived here.

I closed my eyes, and my fingers instantly found my stomach as the memories of Clint and the night I lost our baby flashed in my eyes.

I hated this town.

"Let me grab something from the back." Abigail's voice grew louder as the door began to open.

I slunk further against the wall to protect myself from any wandering eyes. Abigail flipped on the light and shut the door. She frowned as she glanced around the room, but as soon as she saw me, her eyes widened. "You okay?" she asked.

I nodded. "I don't think she knows I'm here."

Abigail offered me a quick nod. "She has no clue. That woman is so wrapped up in her own life. Something about Jack's new wife not wanting to come visit." Abigail met my gaze.

I frowned. "Jack got married?"

"Do you know him? Missy hasn't stopped lamenting his new wife being a pain." She crossed her arms. "What's the story there?"

I shifted my weight as the whole Hodges family tree came rushing back to me. "Missy and her husband Harold had four kids. Jack is her oldest. He's six years older than me and we didn't run in the same circles. Sounds like he finally settled down. I can only imagine what that woman is thinking now that Missy is her mother-in-law. Then there's Cassie, who is eighteen months younger then Jack." I tapped my middle finger as I assigned a family member to each finger. "Same story with her as with Jack. Both doing their own thing when I was growing up."

"That's two."

I nodded, my emotions crawling up my throat once more. I didn't want to utter Clint's name again, but I really didn't have a choice. "There's Clint, who is...my ex. And his younger sister is Claire. She's the baby of the family and has always struggled with Missy."

Abigail studied me. I knew she saw my reaction to saying Clint's name. She knew something, but not everything. When I talked about my past, I kept it to generalizations, nothing too deep.

But I knew that wasn't going to last long.

"So, is there drama between Claire and Missy? I think she mumbled something under her breath about Claire refusing to come as well."

I shrugged. "I don't know, but I wouldn't be surprised if there is." Then I swallowed. If Claire was coming back, did that mean Clint was too? "Did she mention any other family members suddenly making a trip home?"

Abigail shook her head. "Nope. Just those two." She sighed. "I'm pretty sure if she had more things to complain about, she wouldn't be shy in telling me."

I snorted. "Tell me about it."

Abigail reached out and tapped the pad of paper I was clutching. "Why don't you head to Godwins and grab what we need. Missy was hunkering down to tell me some stories, so I'm pretty sure she's going to be here a while."

I glanced down at the list and then back up at Abigail. "I can do that."

She smiled. "Great. It'll probably be a half an hour, but if she's still here after that, I'll send you a text."

I grabbed my purse, which I'd stashed on the back shelf earlier, and slung the strap over my shoulder. "Sounds like a plan."

Abigail nodded before she turned to grab a giant bag

of coffee grounds. She must have seen my confused look as she hoisted it up onto her hip. "I have to come back with something or Missy will suspect somethings off," she said as she patted the bag.

I nodded and then sandwiched myself between two shelves while she slipped out. Now alone, I moved to the back of the shop and pulled open the door. A dark figure suddenly straightened, causing me to let out a squeak.

My eyes widened as a man with dark hair and dark eyes stared down at me. I had half a mind to sprint back through the shop screaming, "Call the cops!" until I remembered who was in the store at that very moment.

And no matter who this man was or what he was doing, he wasn't as scary as Missy Hodges.

"Sorry to scare you," he murmured as he leaned down and picked up a box. Then he flipped open a razor blade and pressed it to the tape that held the box flaps together.

"It's okay," I whispered, my heart pounding harder than I cared to admit.

His dark hair fell over one eye once more, shielding him from sight. I thought about asking if he was new here, but then felt stupid. After all, I was just as new as any newcomer. How was I to know if he was new or not?

He didn't seem to want to engage in conversation, so I just sidestepped him and headed down the alleyway that connected to Main Street. I peeked over my shoulder at him before I turned the corner. He was breaking down the last box and stacking it on top of the others. I glanced around at the back doors of the other shops but couldn't figure out if he belonged to any of them. Or if he was just a good Samaritan, helping out.

I shook my head as my gaze dropped to the sidewalk, and I hurried in the direction of Godwin's. I knew where Missy and Miles were. So it was safe for me to move around downtown for now.

However, I was keenly aware that I didn't know how long my safety would last. I was going to buy what Abigail needed and then hurry back to her bookstore and wait in the back room until the coast was clear.

I must have looked windblown when I walked through the sliding doors at Godwin's. A much older, white-haired version of the Betty Godwin I remembered was standing behind the register, and she froze when she saw me. Her eyes were wide and her lips parted. She held a box of crackers suspended in the air right above the scanner. Like my presence had totally fixed her to the spot. "As I live and breathe," she whispered, loud enough for the woman whose groceries Betty was scanning to turn and look at me.

Not wanting to enter into a conversation of "where've you been?" "you look just like your mother" and "your grandmother never stopped talking about you," I nodded in her direction as I hurried down the first aisle, gripping the list Abigail gave me like it was my life support.

In my confusion with Miles, I seemed to have forgotten I was known around this town. I'd kept to myself when I first returned, and most of the residents of Harmony Island had yet to see me.

It wasn't like I was celebrity or anything, but I was notorious. And with my grandmother's passing, a lot of memories about the inn, my grandmother, and me were dredged to the surface. It didn't help that I was the estranged granddaughter of one of the town's most beloved residents. People always talked and made assumptions. I just hated that they were comments made about me.

Speed was essential if I was going to get out of here before I ran into anyone else I knew on Harmony Island. I just needed to grab the food and get out. Luckily, I found an abandoned cart stashed next to the canned beans. After glancing around to make sure it didn't belong to anyone, I wrapped my hands around the cool metal and began the search for the items on my list.

Thankfully, the items were straightforward and Godwin's was just like everything else in this town—reluctant to change. In a matter of ten minutes, I was rolling up to the register and placing the groceries on the belt.

Betty wasn't shy about staring at me. She stood there with her arms crossed, watching me load the items. Once my cart was empty, she took the carton of creamer and scanned it.

"I was wondering how long it was going to take you to come see me," she said, the beeping of the register filling the awkward air between us.

"Yeah, sorry, ma'am," I said, not really sure where she

was going with this. But my southern upbringing told me I needed to be polite.

Betty stared at me from over her glasses. "So you have to be here for six months, huh?"

I pinched my lips together and nodded. "That's what Gran wanted."

Betty sighed as she rested the bunch of bananas on the scale and typed the number into her computer. "Charlotte always had the last word, didn't she."

"Yeah." A familiar ache rose up in my stomach at the mention of my grandmother. I doubted that feeling would ever go away. And if I were honest with myself, I was starting to get used to it.

It was as if my body refused to forget her. In a way, I was keeping her alive inside of me. Despite our history being what it was, the last thing I wanted to do was forget the woman who raised me. Especially since I knew I still had things to work through.

I must have stayed quiet for too long because when I turned my attention back to Betty, she was studying me. I offered her a weak smile. "Gran was always a character."

Betty's eyes narrowed before she nodded. "She really was." She scanned the last item and then called off the total. I handed her a few twenties, which she took, and then she gathered the change.

I held out my hand, but she hovered hers above it. "Do me a favor," she said.

I glanced up at her. "Yeah?"

She dropped the change into my open palm. "Don't be a stranger around here. I know what Charlotte wanted for you, and it wasn't to be in your hometown alone." She grabbed the receipt and handed it over. "We can let bygones be bygones. Besides, you were so good to my Juniper when you were living here, it's the least I can do."

I studied her, my emotions rising up in my chest from her words. "Really?"

She nodded before handing me a water bottle from the drink display behind her. "Really."

I took the bottle, thanked her, and then hurried out of the store with the groceries in hand. Thankfully, when I got back to Abigail's, Missy was gone.

Abigail happily chatted with me while she put the food away. I just stood off to the side, sipping my water and trying to dissect my feelings.

It was strange to have someone from my past treat me kindly. Especially Betty Godwin. I may have stolen a few too many candy bars from her store when I was younger. Sure, I'd taken her daughter under my wing in high school when I was a senior and she was a freshman. I just didn't think that would make up for the havoc I'd wreaked on the residents of this town.

The fact that she wanted to put the past behind us and show me kindness...it was strange.

And I wasn't sure I was ready to unpack this yet.

If I got too attached to this town, it was going to be hard to leave. And leaving was my fate. Packing up and driving out of town once more was as inevitable as the sun rising in the morning.

Harmony Island wasn't my future. It was my past that I had to relive until my six months were up. And then I would put it behind me like I did so many years ago.

Harmony Island and I were like oil and water. No matter how hard you shook the bottle, they were never meant to mix.

I needed to remember that.

5

BASH

SWEET TEA &
SOUTHERN GENTLEMAN

I DON'T KNOW why I did this to myself.

Somehow, I went out for a walk and ended up at The Shop Around the Corner for the millionth time. I couldn't get Abigail out of my head. I'd been hooked in the brain and I couldn't get her out of my mind.

The harder I fought my desire to see her dark brown hair or her eyes that crinkled at the corners, the weaker I became. It was idiotic to think that the solution to my problem was daydreaming about the woman I was trying to forget.

Every time I headed out of Anders' apartment for the day, I seemed to find my way right back here. Lurking in the shadows of Abigail's shop.

I leaned against the exterior of the bookstore and took a deep breath. I'd contemplated going in to get a coffee, but she seemed to be having a moment with her friend, and I didn't want to interrupt that. Plus, I'd be lying if I said I wasn't grateful that her friend was there.

I needed someone to stop me from making a fool of myself once more.

Abigail had to know that I wanted to be around her. Even though I tried to be discreet, she always seemed to find me. My cheeks heated when I remembered the afternoon that I'd lost my crap in her shop. I thought I'd gotten over reacting like that.

A product from my childhood that I couldn't seem to shake. The fear. The trauma. It always seemed to creep up around me, plaguing me. I'd lost myself to drinking for years. Living in hellhole apartments, trying to forget what happened. What I did. What happened to...

I shook my head as I closed my eyes and tipped my face toward the sky. I'd promised myself I would stop thinking about him. That was my past. And the only way I was going to live some semblance of a life was by pushing what had happened to the darkest corners of my mind and burying it there.

If I didn't... I wasn't sure what I would do.

My phone vibrated in my pocket, startling me. I pushed off the wall and slunk into the shadows of the alley behind the shop. Once I was a few yards away from the bookstore, I pulled my phone out and glanced down.

It was an unknown number.

My finger lingered over the decline button, but something inside of me told me to answer. Maybe it was

Anders. He was coming home soon. He could be in trouble.

Despite my better judgement, I pressed the talk button and brought my phone to my cheek. "Hello?"

Silence.

I glanced down, just to make sure that I'd indeed answered the phone, only to see the seconds ticking up. I brought the phone back, feeling stupid—this was obviously a telemarketer. There was always a pause after answering before they spoke. I moved to hang up, but then I heard a familiar voice that caused my entire body to freeze.

"Sebastian?"

I blinked. No. There was no way they'd found me.

"I know you're there. Just talk to me." The male voice was frantic, causing my heart to pound in my chest.

I shook my head as I pressed the end call button and slipped the phone back into my pocket. I couldn't believe it. All of these years of hiding. Of switching addresses and phones. Only to have them track me down.

Apparently, my disappearance had become a game for them. One they seemed relentless to win.

I hurried toward the center of town, my phone buzzing in my pocket as I went. The first two were phone calls, and the last was a text message. I zeroed in on the cellphone store, pulled open the glass door, and barreled inside.

An elderly woman was on her way out, and I nearly ran her over.

"Sorry," I murmured as I ducked my head and moved toward the employee, a woman in her mid-twenties, who looked both startled by my sudden appearance and concerned that the elderly woman was okay.

"We'll see you later, Ms. Thompson," she called out.

Ms. Thompson nodded before she shot me an annoyed look and pushed the door open. I placed my hands on the counter and stared up at the worker who was now watching me with wide eyes.

"Can I help you?" she asked.

I nodded as I glanced down at her name tag. "Yes, please, Elizabeth." I knocked on the glass. "I need a new phone."

She studied me. "Are you looking to upgrade?"

I shook my head. "No. I need a new phone. New number. New...everything." She didn't move. She looked afraid that I would attack her at any moment, so I forced a smile. "Please."

She didn't relax, but my smile seemed to ease her fears enough for her to come out from behind the counter. "Um, sure. What phone are you looking for?"

"Something I can pay cash for."

She side-eyed me.

I shrugged, hoping to come off as quirky instead of creepy. "I just don't like big government spying on me." I forced a laugh.

She paused and then nodded. "That's not the first time I've heard that today."

"Oh really?"

A soft smile emerged as she brought me over to the prepaid phones. "Although, I hear it mostly from the older generation. Not someone like..." Her voice trailed off as her cheeks flushed.

I was flattered, but in no way interested. "I have an old soul."

Her eyes widened before she let out a soft giggle and pulled a phone from the wall display. "This one seems to get the best reception here on the island. It's a decent phone for this price." She handed it over to me. "I think you're really going to like this one."

I nodded as I flipped the packaging over a few times in my hands and then handed it back to her. "I'll take it."

She brought me over to the cash register and rang me up. Once we were done, she slipped it into a bag and handed it over. "Do you need me to help you set it up?"

I shook my head as I took it from her. "Naw, this isn't my first time."

She nodded. "Well, I hope you can keep big government off your back."

I gave her quick smile. "Me too."

I could tell that she wanted to keep talking, but I wasn't interested. Instead, I gave her a nod and slipped out of the shop. I rounded the corner and leaned against the building as I ripped open the packaging. In no time, I'd set the phone up.

I shot Anders a quick text letting him know that I had

a new phone and that my old number was no longer going to work. He replied with a thumbs-up emoji. I nodded to myself as I tucked my new phone into my back pocket. It was nice to have a friend who understood my situation. Who wasn't shocked when I switched numbers every other month.

Anders had a vague understanding as to why I was running. We never went into details about it, and he knew that I wasn't interested in sharing my situation beyond surface facts. And he was okay with that. We both had demons in our past that we wanted to keep hidden, and it sort of bonded us together as friends.

We could live our lives without either of us forcing the other to face his past.

With my new phone set up, I pulled out my old one. I flipped it around in my hand a few times. The desire to stomp on it without reading the text fought against the desire to see what Nicholas wanted.

I would recognize the voice of my father's right-hand man anywhere. He'd been there when I was born, and was more my father than the man I was genetically related to. Whatever he had to say, I didn't want to hear it.

I'd written off my family and my father the night...

I shook my head. No. Nothing good came from thinking about my family or the life I'd left. I was done with all of that. The best thing I could do for everyone involved was just to stay away.

Determination rose up inside of me as I set the phone

down on the ground and then smashed it with my foot. After giving it a few good stomps, I dropped the phone in a nearby garbage and walked away.

Relief filled my chest. Sure, Nicholas had been able to find one of my many numbers, but that trail was going to run cold for him. Besides, I hadn't been on the call long enough for him to trace where I was. And if he finally figured it out, I would be long gone. Anders had a few weeks left here, but that didn't mean I had to stay.

There was nothing keeping me here.

My gaze drifted in the direction of The Shop Around the Corner. A sour feeling rose up in my gut at the thought of walking away, but that was quickly replaced with the feeling of determination. After all, my life was a mess. I wasn't in a place to start anything with any woman, much less the woman that my friend was interested in.

The best thing I could do for her and myself was to end this infatuation right here, right now. After all, if I decided to pursue a relationship with her—even a platonic one—I wasn't sure what would happen if my family found out.

I'd been around long enough to know that relationships with me would never work. It was better for her to be interested in Anders. His life was simpler than mine.

By a lot.

I shoved my hands into the front of my hoodie as I headed down the sidewalk and made my way to the apartment I shared with Anders. Once inside, I shut and locked the front door, dropped my keys on the counter, and headed to my room.

I flopped down on my bed and glanced around. The room was empty besides a TV on the dresser and a few dirty clothes in the corner. It didn't make sense to collect or display anything, I never lingered anywhere longer than a few weeks.

I reached over to the nightstand and grabbed the remote. I needed the distraction mind-numbing TV would bring. The glow from the TV lit up the dark room. I flipped through a few channels before I landed on a news channel, and my entire body went numb.

There, on the screen, was the image of my father in a hospital bed, with tubes hooked up to his body. Just below it the words, *near death,* scrolled past on the chyron.

That had been the reason for Nicholas' call. He wanted to let me know that my father was ill.

All of these years running, and my former life was bound to catch up with me. My father might be dying. And even though I wanted to ignore it, I couldn't forget it now that it was staring me in the face.

There was a chance I was going to have to go home and face my past. My history was never going to die. No matter how much I wanted it to.

I was who I was, and there was nothing I could do about it.

6

MILES

SHELBY SPENT the entire day away from the inn. I hated that every time I heard a car pulling up to the inn, I dropped whatever I was doing to look out the nearest window...just to be disappointed.

Dinner rolled around, and the few guests the inn had were sitting down to the pork roast with mixed vegetables that I'd made up. I was exhausted. Belle was sitting in her highchair in the kitchen, eating her food and giggling at the show I'd set up for her to watch on her tablet.

I leaned back in the chair, extending out my legs and letting my body relax. I wanted to talk to Shelby. To reassure her that everything was okay. That I was here and I was committed.

But I knew that I couldn't do that.

She'd asked me to stay away, so I was going to respect

that. Plus, I still needed to talk to Tamara, and she'd spent most of the day in her room.

Mrs. Porter had shown up this morning to watch Belle, which gave me just enough time to hurry over to Shelby and let her rip my heart out. When I got back to the inn, Mrs. Porter offered to take Belle to the park, which left me and Tamara alone. But Tamara must have sensed that I was in a mood, because she exclaimed that she was exhausted and hurried up to her room where she stayed all afternoon.

I kept busy cleaning rooms, doing laundry, and prepping for dinner. But now that all my chores were done, I was a mess. I needed something to distract me from Shelby's absence and my breaking heart.

Belle's squeal drew my attention back to her, and I couldn't help but smile. She had gravy around her lips and a mouth full of potatoes, but she was happy. And that was all that mattered to me.

"Knock knock?" a smooth voice asked as the kitchen's door slowly opened.

I hated that my heart picked up speed at the sound of a feminine voice. I knew it wasn't Shelby, but my body responded with excitement anyway.

Tamara peeked around the door and offered me a weak smile. "Hey," she whispered. "Is it okay if I come in?"

My gaze drifted over to Belle. Even though I wanted to protect my daughter from her mother who might not stick around, I also knew that it wasn't my right to keep them apart. And right now, I had the ability to control the situation. It was on my terms.

I nodded, and Tamara's eyes widened as if she hadn't expected me to say yes. She hesitated and then pushed through the door and into the kitchen. Her gaze drifted to Belle. But she pulled it away and sat down across from me, where her gaze drifted over to Belle once more.

Belle seemed unfazed by her mother's presence. She continued to eat her dinner and laugh at her show. Tamara relaxed back against her chair, all the while keeping her gaze trained on her daughter.

"She's so big," Tamara whispered.

I nodded. "She is."

Tamara glanced over at me, her eyes full of tears. "I can't believe I missed all of that."

Her statement made me uncomfortable, so I shifted on my seat. "Yeah. That's what happens when you've been gone for two years."

Her smile faltered and I felt guilty. I knew she was struggling, but that didn't change the fact that she'd abandoned her daughter. It was my job to hold her accountable so that my daughter stayed safe.

"Is she walking?"

I nodded.

"Talking?"

I paused. A few do-gooders around town had expressed concern at her lack of speech, but I just brushed them off. Charlotte had said that each kid grew at different rates and to just be patient, she'd get there.

"We're working on it."

Tamara didn't seem concerned, which helped steel my nerves against my own fears. Belle's lack of speech was probably normal, and I had nothing to worry about. At least, that was what I was going to repeat in my mind every time my nerves got the better of me.

"I just can't get over how beautiful she is," Tamara said, her smile returning to her lips as her gaze never left Belle's face.

"She's beautiful," I repeated, smiling as well. We must have been a sight, the two of us just staring at Belle and grinning like idiots. But I loved that girl more than I loved anything else. She was easy to love. It felt as natural as breathing.

A surge of protection coursed through my chest as my gaze drifted over to Tamara, wondering if she felt the same. Questions floated through my mind. What were her plans now that she was here? I needed to know her angle before I was going to allow her to be a part of Belle's life again.

"So what's your plan here?" I asked as I tapped my fingers on the table.

That seemed to snap Tamara from her trance. She turned her attention to me, and when her gaze met mine, her smile slowly disappeared. "With Belle?" she asked as she leaned back in her chair.

"Belle. Harmony Island...me." Shelby's words drifted back into my mind. She wanted me to give Tamara a chance. If we could make it as a family, she wanted me to take that route.

It left me wondering, did Tamara want the same?

Tamara shrugged. "I want to stay sober. I want to heal. I want a relationship with my daughter..." Her voice trailed off as her gaze slowly rose to meet mine.

"And me?"

She pinched her lips as she studied me. There was so much mystery in her eyes, and it made me feel uncomfortable. Fear filled my chest.

The truth was, I loved Shelby. I always had. But if Tamara wanted to make it work...could I walk away from that? Belle deserved the best life, and her mother was an integral part of that.

"Miles..." She sighed. "I don't know what to say to that. We have a rocky past, we do." She closed her eyes. "I would be lying if I said there weren't times that I thought about us getting back together. What life would be like if we gave us another chance." She opened her eyes and her gaze met mine.

I could tell that she was searching for an answer. Wondering if I felt that way too.

She reached out and rested her hand on mine. "Do you feel the same?"

My gaze drifted down to her hand. The warmth from her palm and the feeling of her touch shocked me. I wasn't sure what to do, but the sound of the screen door slamming had me jerking my hand away.

I pushed away from the table and stood, my gaze whipping over to the door just in time to see Shelby's brown hair disappear into the darkness.

I didn't think—I acted. I crossed the kitchen and pulled open the door. Tamara and Belle could be alone for a minute. I needed to fix this before Shelby packed her bags and left for New York once more.

"Shelby!" I yelled as I jogged across the gravel driveway and beat her to the door of the cottage. I pressed my hand against the wood, stopping her from pulling it open and disappearing inside.

Shelby shook her head as she kept her hands firmly on the door handle. "Let me go inside," she whispered. Tears were flowing down her cheeks and her voice was hoarse.

My heart ached as I studied her. "Nothing happened. We were just talking about Belle and got nostalgic. I didn't want to hold her hand."

Shelby stopped trying to pull the door open and just stood there. Fearing that she'd gone into shock, I dipped down to study her. Her eyes were closed.

"I'm moving in with Abigail," she whispered.

I blinked. "What?"

"I'm moving in with Abigail," she said again, this time more forceful. "I can't...be here." She took in a deep breath, the last two words coming out a whisper.

"You can't be here?"

She nodded and then tipped her face back at the same time she opened her eyes. My heart pounded as I saw the pain and resolve there.

"Why? Just stay here. It'll be fine." I was moments from getting down on my knees and begging her not to leave. I needed her here. I needed to know that I hadn't ruined everything. That there was still a chance she could love me like I loved her.

Shelby shook her head. "I've decided. It's what's best for me." She swallowed as she dropped her gaze to the ground and then brought it slowly back up to meet mine. "It's what's best for you and Belle."

"It's not what's best for me," I said, my voice lowering so my words came out in a growl. I wanted her to stop talking. She didn't know what was best for me or my daughter. I needed her in my life. I wasn't anyone without her.

She reached out to touch me. Her fingers lingering inches from my arm. But then she stopped and dropped her hand once more. "You'll regret us, eventually. You'll regret not giving you and Tamara a chance. She's trying to change. She wants to be a family."

I shook my head. "You don't know that."

She gave me an annoyed look. "I could tell by the way she looked at you. You're an anchor for her." Shelby wrapped her arms around her chest and took in a deep breath. "This is your family and you need to fight for it." She took a step back. It was taking all of my strength not to reach out and pull her against me. To hold her so she could never leave me.

"Shelby, I..." I couldn't figure out what I needed to say to get her to stay. She seemed so resolute in her decision, and I feared that anything I said would just push her further away.

"How long will you be at Abigail's?" The words tasted bitter in my mouth, but I said them anyway. She needed me to support her. And even though it broke my heart, I was going to be here for her.

"I don't know. I'll be leaving next weekend for a few days. Abigail said I could work at the bookstore, helping out." She took in a deep breath and then let out the air slowly. "It's what's best. I'll get out of your hair so you and Tamara can figure out what the future looks like for you."

I wanted to reject her declaration. Being away from her wasn't what was right, but I wasn't going to push her. Pushing Shelby always resulted in the exact opposite of what I wanted. Last time, it resulted in her packing up and leaving for ten years. There had been only one person who could bring her back, and she was gone.

There was nothing keeping Shelby here. I'd hoped that I could be that anchor for her, but that chance was quickly slipping away from me.

I was done with living my life where Shelby ran away to New York. So, if she needed to be at Abigail's to heal, I was going to count that as a blessing and leave it at that. I swallowed and shoved my hands into the front pockets of my jeans as I took a step back.

"Can I help you pack a suitcase?"

Shelby rubbed her upper arms as she shook her head. "I, um..." She took in another deep breath. "I'll be okay. It's not like I have a ton of stuff." She glanced around. "I'll probably leave some of it here, if that's okay. I'm not sure how much space Abigail has. I don't want to overwhelm her."

I nodded even though every part of my body was rejecting what she was saying. "That's fine. I won't do anything with the cottage. You take your time, and the door is always open."

Her lips tipped up into a small smile as she nodded. "Sounds good."

My heart was breaking, and the last thing I wanted was for her to see it. So I turned and jogged a few feet before Shelby's voice stopped me.

"Hey, Miles?"

I stopped and glanced over my shoulder. "Yeah?"

She frowned as she studied me. "Thanks for being there for me when I came back. I really couldn't have dealt with the will without your help."

I raised my hand and shook my head. "You don't need to thank me. I'll always be here for you when you need me."

She held my gaze before nodding. "I know. Thanks."

I just stood there, studying her. I didn't want to break

the connection between us. The minute I turned and walked away, things would be over. Any hope I had that we could be a family, that Shelby could love me like I loved her, would disappear, and I'd be left alone once more.

Her lips tipped up into a small smile before she turned and disappeared into the cottage. I stood there, staring at the dark wood door, praying that she would open it and run into my arms, where I would hold her and never let her go.

But time ticked by and nothing happened. The cottage was quiet, and there was no sign that she regretted what she'd said. Dejected, I made my way back to the inn. I shut the door behind me as I walked into the kitchen.

Tamara had pulled her chair up next to Belle and lifted her gaze to meet mine.

"Everything okay?" she asked.

I swallowed hard against the emotions in my throat as I shook my head. "No." Then I sucked in my breath and tipped my face to the ceiling. If I was going to survive, I needed to push my emotions as far down as I possibly could.

That was how I got through most of my life, and right now was no different.

Shelby had broken my heart once more. It was like fate was trying to tell me to move on, that we weren't destined to be together. That our relationship was only going to end in heartbreak, over and over again.

I was the stupid sap that kept ignoring fate. But I was done having a broken heart. I was done fighting the inevitable.

Fate had finally won.

Shelby and I were over.

Forever.

7

ABIGAIL

SWEET TEA &
SOUTHERN GENTLEMAN

SABRINA WENT to bed as soon as I got home. Samuel was awake and hungry, but Sabrina didn't wait for me to take off my shoes much less give me a rundown on his day. Instead, she handed him off to me and disappeared into her room, where she promptly fell asleep.

After feeding Samuel, I gave him a bath. While he was in the warm water, happily splashing around, my phone rang.

I dried my hands before pressing the phone between my cheek and shoulder. "Hello?"

"Abigail?"

I frowned. I recognized the female voice, but I hadn't bothered to look to see who was calling. "Yeah, this is she."

"It's Shelby."

I felt stupid that I hadn't recognized her voice. "Hey, Shelby. What's up?"

There was a pause. Then a soft sob. "I'm outside of your building right now. Can I..." Another sob. "Can I come up?"

I straightened and looked toward the living room as if I could see through walls. "You're at my building?"

There was a rustling sound as if her chin was brushing the microphone before she whimpered, "Yes."

I reached over and grabbed Samuel's towel and laid it on the plush bathmat at my feet. "Let me get Samuel out of the bath and I'll buzz you up."

"Thanks," she whispered before another sniffle sounded through the speaker.

Samuel cooed as I wrapped the towel around him and then hurried to the intercom system and buzzed Shelby up. It only took her a few minutes to get to my door. I pulled it open as soon as I heard a knock and then waved her inside.

Shelby looked like a mess. Her nose was red and her eyes were bloodshot. It was as if she'd been crying for hours.

"Follow me," I instructed as I led her into Samuel's room. I laid Samuel down on his changing table and began dressing him. Shelby stayed close to the door, her gaze downturned as if she were waiting for an invitation to come in and relax.

"You can sit there if you want," I said as I pulled the strap to Samuel's diaper and nodded toward the rocking chair in the corner.

Shelby didn't say anything. Instead, she just collapsed in the chair, which rocked a few times from the impact. I waited to see if she was going to tell me why she was here, but she didn't seem that motivated to explain.

So I just cooed and sang to Samuel while I dressed him in dinosaur footie pajamas and brushed his hair a bit before picking him up and resting him against my shoulder. I bounced him a few times before turning around to focus on Shelby.

"Want some tea?" I asked.

Shelby looked more put together than she had when she first got here. Her tears had dried up, and she wrapped her arms around her chest as she nodded.

"Yeah, that would be good," she whispered.

She followed me back into the kitchen, where I set Samuel in his highchair. Then I moved around, gathering the tea bag options and starting water warming in a kettle on the stove.

Shelby settled onto the barstool, rested her elbows on the counter, and watched me. Once the water was heating and our tea was picked out, I draped the strings down the front of the mugs and then turned my attention to her.

"So, are we going to talk about why you're here?" I asked, offering her a soft smile. I had an inkling, but I wanted to hear it from her.

She sighed, grabbed a tissue from the box next to her, and fiddled with the corner. "I just had to get out of there."

She took in a deep breath. "There's no way I can stay there with Tamara spending time there too."

I nodded. I understood why she was so frustrated. I hated that she was going through this. If I could fix it for her, I would. But my life was a mess, and if I couldn't get my own crap together, how was I going to help Shelby?

Shelby paused as she looked around. "I hate to ask you this, but is there any way...?"

"Do you need to stay here?" I asked, hoping that if I said it first, she'd feel less awkward.

Her gaze met mine for a moment before she nodded. "If you don't mind. Just until I leave for my trip. I'll work on finding a small place to move into while I wait out this ridiculous will stipulation." She blew out her breath. "All I know is I can't stay at the inn. Not when..." Tears filled her eyes once more, and she pressed her cheekbones as if to keep them at bay.

"I totally understand," I said as I reached across the counter and patted her hand. "You can stay here as long as you need. You can have my room, and I'll just sleep in Samuel's." At the mention of his name, Samuel smiled a huge, happy grin. I couldn't help but respond by smiling back. "I'm up most mornings with him anyway," I said under my breath, more for me than for Shelby. But she heard and her gaze drifted around the apartment.

"Where's Sabrina?"

I sighed as the kettle on the stove began to whistle.

"She's tired. Dropped him in my arms as soon as I got home before hurrying off to hide in her room." Guilt washed over me as I caught sight of my nephew. Truth was, I loved that kid and would do anything for him. I just wished his mother felt the same.

Not wanting to wallow in my struggles, I pushed my feelings as far down as I could before turning to Shelby and offering her a smile. "Enough about me, tell me what happened when you went home."

I had some idea of what was happening between Shelby and Miles. She'd told me that his ex was back and that she needed a job to get away from whatever his baby momma's return meant. I just hadn't thought she'd run away. Something must have happened to push her to that point.

She started talking, telling me about walking in on them in the kitchen, her running to the cottage, and Miles sprinting after her. I could tell that she loved the man. Her expression turned sorrowful as she spoke about what he said and how she reacted.

I filled her mug with hot water as she recounted how it felt to stand there and tell him that she was leaving. That they were over. And how it broke her heart to pack her bags, dump them into the trunk of her car, and see him standing on the porch of the inn as she drove away.

Once she was done, she held the mug of steaming tea between two hands, gingerly taking a tiny sip before puckering her lips and setting the mug in her lap.

"So that's it?" I asked as I leaned my hip against the counter.

"It has to be. I mean, we really have no other choice."

I studied her, biting back my response. She had a choice. She was just choosing the wrong one. I wanted to say something. To convince her that walking away wasn't going to soothe the pain she had built up inside. But I feared that if I pushed her too hard, she would walk away from me too.

She was vulnerable and hurting, and right now all she needed was a friend. I was going to be that for her. If I couldn't lessen Sabrina's pain, maybe I could make a dent in Shelby's.

"Well, maybe some time away will help. And your trip with..." I raised my eyebrows.

"Titan."

"Titan will be just what you need to forget how you're feeling."

She paused, and for a moment I feared I'd over-stepped. I was trying to be supportive and encouraging, but I also didn't want her to feel like I was attacking Miles. Living with Sabrina after Trevor left her made me acutely aware of how protective women could be even when their significant others were bums who didn't deserve the women who were protecting them.

When Shelby nodded, a wave of relief washed through me. I hadn't overstepped like I'd feared.

"It's for the best," Shelby whispered as she brought the

rim of her mug to her lips and took a sip. I wasn't sure if it was for me or for her own sanity, but I figured she wasn't waiting for a response from me, so I just turned my focus to Samuel.

We kept our conversation light as I popped some popcorn and we spent the night watching FRIENDS reruns until we started to fall asleep. Samuel was passed out in his rocker and I didn't want to move him, so I waved toward my bedroom and told Shelby to have at it. I was going to sleep on the couch for tonight.

She nodded and then padded down the hallway and disappeared into my room. It didn't take long for my eyelids to grow heavy and for me to pass out.

IT WAS nice to have someone help around the house in the morning. We worked together making breakfast and getting Samuel settled. Sabrina looked startled when she saw Shelby moving around the kitchen, but she didn't say anything. Instead, she just plopped down on the couch and waved toward Samuel's swing when I approached her with him.

Hating that he was probably going to spend the day in that swing, I contemplated asking her to take more of an active role with him, but I bit that comment back. She was up and semi-dressed. I was going to take that as a win today.

Shelby followed after me as I led her through the building and out to my car. When we got to the shop, I unlocked the back door and paused.

Someone had broken down all of the boxes that I'd thrown out here yesterday. "That's strange," I muttered under my breath.

"What?" Shelby asked.

I jumped a little, forgetting that I wasn't out here alone. "The boxes," I said, nodding toward the neat stack of flattened cardboard.

"I saw some guy breaking them down yesterday."

I stopped. "Some guy?"

She nodded. "I didn't recognize him, but then again, I wouldn't recognize anyone here." She frowned. "I figured he ran one of these other shops."

I glanced around the alley, wondering who it might be. In all the years I'd worked here at the bookstore, no one had ever broken down my boxes for me. "Maybe someone is visiting," I said as I held open the door and waved Shelby in.

"Yeah, probably. With me here, though, I can do all that work. I expect you to run me into the ground just for the distraction."

I nodded as I followed after her. "You better be careful. You'll spoil me with all of this help. And when you leave, I won't know what to do with myself."

Shelby slipped into my office and emerged tying on an apron. "Well, maybe you can convince me to stay," she said with the first genuine smile I'd seen from her in a long time.

I quirked an eyebrow. "Don't tempt me."

We laughed before I asked her to start baking some blueberry muffins while I worked on the inventory. With the two of us working, we were going to get a lot of my daily tasks done early. It was nice.

The morning went smoothly. The construction workers came in like clockwork. Even Missy stopped by, but thankfully Shelby saw her come in and slipped into my office before she was discovered.

Missy was in a hurry. Some gossip emergency had her grabbing a coffee and muffin to go. Once she was gone, Shelby came out of the office, looking a little pale but relieved.

"Did she know I was here?" Shelby asked as she leaned against the counter with her arms folded.

I shook my head. "I don't think so. If she did, she didn't say anything. She looked preoccupied with whoever was on the other side of the phone."

Shelby nodded but then stilled as her gaze focused on the ground in front of her. I could tell she was working through something. And I wanted to help, I did, but I didn't know what to say. So instead, I walked over to her and wrapped my arm around her shoulders, and we stood there in silence.

Whatever her future looked like, I wanted her to know

that I was here. We were friends and I was going to help her through anything. I may not be able to fix all the broken parts of my life, but I was going to do my best to help her with hers.

8

BASH

SWEET TEA &
SOUTHERN GENTLEMAN

I FELT PRETTY good about myself. I spent the last few days holed up in my apartment, fighting the urge to see Abigail, but not actually acting on it. It was the first seventy-two hours that I'd gone without seeing her, and despite the fact that I was mind-numbingly bored, I was dang proud of myself.

Perhaps, I could live my life without seeing her and survive.

I sighed as I clicked off the TV, and my room went dark. I'd filled the time I spent here watching reruns of public court episodes in between falling asleep on my bed.

If I were honest with myself, I knew I couldn't keep living like this. But there was no way I could get a job or even risk living my life in a big city. I didn't want anything to do with my father or the life he wanted me to have, so the best thing I could do was stay in the shadows.

And I was getting used to it, even though I was starting to lose who I was in all of this.

The sound of keys jingling at the front door had me sitting up. I swung my feet off the bed and stood, excitement brewing inside of me. I was ready to have someone to talk to that wasn't my reflection or the lone picture of a cowboy that had been left by a previous tenant.

The lock released as soon as I rounded the corner, and the door was pushed open. Anders was dragging his suitcase behind him and startled when he saw me. I must have looked like a mess because his eyes instantly widened as he took me in.

"What..." He swallowed as he brought the back of his wrist up to his nose and recoiled. "When was the last time you showered?"

I shrugged as I moved to take his suitcase. "I don't remember."

Anders held his suitcase firmly as he took a step back. "I've got it, man." Then he moved to peer around the corner. "Is there something wrong with the bathroom?"

I pushed my hand through my hair and then winced. "Nope."

He eyed me. "So the water is running. The drains are working." He clicked his tongue. "And the water is hot?"

I shot him an annoyed look. "Geez, I get it. I'll shower." I headed toward my bedroom to get a towel.

"We'll catch up when you're clean," Anders called from behind me.

I waved his words away as I shut the bathroom door behind me and flipped the shower on. Once I was under the hot water, I didn't want to leave. So I lingered, letting the heat permeate my entire body. Stress washed away as I lathered up and rinsed off.

Once I was dry, I wrapped the towel around my waist and opened the door, a steam cloud billowing out into the hall. Anders' bedroom door was open and I could see him lying on his bed next to his half-emptied suitcase. He was scrolling on his phone.

I slipped into my room and dressed. I felt like a new person as I walked back out into the hallway. I was grateful he was home because that not only motivated me to do the things I needed to be doing, but it also meant I wasn't alone.

And things never went well for me when I was alone.

I stood in the doorway of Anders' room, leaning against the doorframe. He finished typing on his phone screen and then set it down on the bed next to him. He smirked when he saw me.

"Feel better?"

I nodded. "Yeah."

"It's a good thing I came home when I did. The neighbors might have called an ambulance thinking someone had died in here."

I folded my arms. "I wasn't that bad."

Anders wrinkled his nose. "My sense of smell begs to differ."

I shook my head and then waved toward his open suitcase before stuffing my hands into my front pockets. "How was your trip this time?" Anders was my best friend. He knew me back when I ran away from the nuclear bomb that was my family life. He hung out with me on the streets as I slipped into addiction. He got his life cleaned up before I did, so there was a bit of time when we didn't talk. But once I was ready to move on with my life and crawl out of the hole I'd dug myself into, he was there to help me out.

I owed the man my life, even though there were times I didn't agree with what he was doing. He said he had trips for work, but I didn't know of any construction company who sent their workers around the country.

Anders tucked his hand behind his head before he leaned back against his headboard. "It was great. Nice to get away but also nice to come back." He glanced over at me. "How's it been here? Holding the fort down with Abigail for me?"

At the mention of Abigail's name, my heart began to pound. Not wanting him to sense a change in me, I just shrugged. "I stopped by there a few times, but she was always busy. Things are hopping here in Harmony."

Anders nodded as he pushed off his bed and stood. "That's what my boss was saying. There's some deep pockets coming to Harmony looking to buy up as much real estate as they can. Something about the southern Martha's Vineyard." He shrugged as he met me in the doorway. "I don't really know, but I'm here for it. I'm ready to make some serious cash." He patted my shoulder as he walked past me.

I followed him into the kitchen.

"What about you? Have you been able to find any work while I've been gone?"

I hated the fact that I was the loser in our friendship. I'd been trying to figure out how to get a job without having to ask for pay under the table. People in Harmony seemed pretty straight-laced, so bringing someone on who wasn't on the books didn't seem like an option they'd consider.

And I feared that if I even asked, that would raise some red flags. "Naw. Not sure how to say, 'any chance you want to hire me without telling the IRS that you hired me?' "

Anders nodded. "Yeah, I can see that. It is a close-knit community." He grabbed a bowl from the cupboard next to the sink. "I'll ask around the site tomorrow. Someone's bound to have heard of something. I can't go into a store without someone backing me into a corner and telling me all about some leaky faucet they have."

Relief flooded me. I hated feeling like I was free-loading off my friend. I wanted to do my part. "Thanks, man."

"Sure." He set the bowl of ramen and water into the microwave and started it. It whirred to life. He pulled his phone from his pocket and swiped it on. "So what was with the new number?" He didn't look up when he asked me.

I shrugged. "Just some people from my past got ahold of it."

He glanced up at me for a second before he turned his focus back to his phone. "As long as they don't come track us down in Harmony..." He didn't finish his sentence, like he was waiting for me to assure him.

I knew he was probably thinking about people who had been wrapped up with my addiction. Little did he know it went deeper than that. "It'll be fine. They aren't going to bother me again."

I waited to see if he picked up on the panicked tone in my voice, but he didn't look up. Instead, he just nodded and continued typing away at his screen. He finished with his text and glanced back up at me once more as he stuffed his phone into his pocket. "Yeah, sure. Sounds good."

The microwave rang and Anders pulled out the ramen and grabbed a fork. He looked so calm. I envied him. He gave me a quick grin as he passed by me. "I'm waiting for Abigail to call me back, so you'll have to excuse me while I eat in my room."

My thoughts were too erratic to process what he'd said. I was just grateful that he was ending this conversation before I went and spilled something that I was going to regret later.

Dad knew that I had no interest in rekindling a relationship. He also knew that I would continue to run from him, his business, and the ridiculous rules that being his son entailed. So even if Nicholas found me again, I'd just run. Leave everything and start over again somewhere else.

I didn't want that. I liked Harmony, and I liked a certain bookstore owner. But I would run. To save my friend. To save this town.

To save a woman I was rapidly caring a little too much about.

I'd walk away from it all, taking the weight of my family with me. Because that was the legacy of being a Torres. I was born with it and I would die with it.

And nothing I could do would change any of that.

9

MILES

IT HAD BEEN seven days since Shelby moved out. I was trying to act like my heart wasn't broken, but I was failing at it. I kept a smile on my face whenever I was with Belle, but as soon as she left the room, the reality of Shelby's departure would surround me. I was finding it hard to be happy.

Tamara seemed to notice. Things between us were tense, but watching her reconnect with her daughter helped lessen the frustration I felt about her return.

I'd laid out some basic rules at the beginning—what I was comfortable with her doing with Belle and what I wasn't. Any time we were together, I was fine with her playing with Belle. But I wasn't to the point where I was comfortable with her taking our daughter out alone.

I still didn't trust that she wouldn't take off and never look back.

Belle always seemed to smile when she played with her mom, and that soothed the father section of my soul. I wanted Tamara and Belle to have a good relationship. I wanted them to know each other and have that mother-daughter bond that I never saw Shelby and her mom have.

But at the same time, seeing Tamara and Belle together caused another part of me to ache.

I'd seen how close Shelby and Belle had gotten, and it broke my heart that Shelby wasn't here to foster that relationship.

I was a mess.

I still wanted Shelby to be a mother-figure for my daughter, but I wanted my daughter's biological mother to be in her life as well. It wasn't fair that I wanted to demand this of both women. But my stomach was in knots, and I lacked the ability to accept whatever outcome was going to come of this.

I was torn and it was eating me up inside. And I was left wanting something to soothe this broken soul of mine.

"You okay?"

Tamara's voice startled me. I was sitting at the kitchen table, mulling over the mess that my life had become. I turned to see her standing in the doorway, studying me.

"Yeah," I said, pushing away from the table so I could rest my elbows on my knees.

Tamara was quiet for a moment before she crossed the room and pulled a chair out from the table. "Belle is down for a nap," she said as she settled onto her seat.

I leaned back against my chair. "That's good."

Silence.

Tamara continued studying me. Then she dropped her gaze to the tabletop and ran her fingers along the grain. "I really want you to know how thankful I am that you let me stay here." I could hear her emotions in her voice. "Spending this last week with Belle has been amazing." She paused before she brought her gaze up to meet mine. "I'm so grateful I get to be a part of her life again."

I nodded. "I'm happy she has her mom back." I leaned forward, forcing Tamara to meet my gaze. "You're a good mom. You've done a lot to clean yourself up. The last thing I would want is to keep you away."

Tears glistened in Tamara's eyes. "Really?"

I nodded as I reached out and rested my hand on hers. "Really."

Tamara's gaze drifted down to our hands. I started to pull away only to stop when her other hand landed on mine.

My whole body froze. Her hand was warm and soft and caused my entire body to react.

What was she doing?

"Tamara—"

"Miles, I was just thinking."

I stopped speaking as I waited for her to continue. Maybe I'd read this wrong. Maybe she was just looking for a friend. We had been physical in the past. What was the rules for physical intimacy for two people who were once in a relationship and had a child together?

She flicked her gaze up to mine before dropping it to our hands. "I was just thinking..." Her voice was soft, almost a whisper, like she feared what she was about to ask.

I knew I should pull back. That I should stop her before she said what I feared she was going to say. But I couldn't. I was frozen, and she looked so vulnerable that I let her continue.

"What if we tried again?"

Those were the words I was worried she would speak. Those five little words ripped at my already fraying emotions. How could I say no to the mother of my daughter? I knew what it was like to be a product of parents who'd split up. Of parents who said it was too hard and walked away from each other.

How could I put my daughter through that?

I cursed under my breath as I pulled my hand away. I wasn't ready to face this. I needed to fix my relationship with Shelby, not focus on what a future might look like with Tamara.

"I can't..." I started, but then let my words trail off. I knew I needed to shut this idea down. First, Shelby had insisted that I give Tamara a chance, and now Tamara was suggesting the same thing.

It was too much. This was too hard.

If I said yes, I'd be breaking Shelby's heart—even

though she gave me permission to pursue this. If I said no, I'd feel like I was ruining my daughter's future. What if Tamara got mad when I rejected her?

How could I explain to my daughter down the road that I had the chance to give her a normal childhood, and I chose not to? I wasn't ready to face any of this.

"Let's just leave things the way they are," I finally managed out. I met Tamara's gaze with the hopes that she would see just how hard her question was for me.

She studied me for a moment and then nodded. "Of course. I didn't mean to upset you. I was just loving being with Belle, so I thought..." Her voice trailed off, and I could see what she was trying to say without actually saying it.

"I know," I said. I hoped that if she understood the thought had crossed my mind as well, she would drop it.

She furrowed her brows and then nodded. "Okay."

Silence fell between us once more.

"Coffee," Tamara said as she pushed her chair out and headed toward the coffee pot.

I wasn't sure what I wanted to do, so I just sat there, watching her make coffee. Her movements were monotonous and mesmerizing, and I couldn't seem to pull my gaze away. When she turned and headed back to the table, her gaze met mine and her brows knit together. I dropped my gaze and cleared my throat.

I wasn't sure what that had been, but the last thing I

wanted was for Tamara to think I was watching her because I was changing my mind.

If she was curious, she didn't say anything as she sat down next to me once more. Then she brought her coffee mug to her lips and smiled at me from over the rim. She set the mug down and then leaned onto her elbows. "So what's the plan for today?"

I shifted on my seat, grateful that we were going to talk about something other than my future with either woman. "I've got some rooms to clean and get ready for new guests tonight. I also have dinner to start." I waved toward the fridge. "I've got a pot roast to throw into the oven."

Tamara glanced toward the fridge. "I could help with that if you want." She shrugged and gave me a soft smile. "It's the least I can do with you letting me stay here."

I studied her. Over the last week, I'd kept her at arm's length, but help sounded nice. I was tired and overworked. Emotionally, I was spent. So having someone else step up sounded like the break I needed.

"Recipe is in the cupboard next to the oven. Gran was meticulous about her recipes, so make sure you follow it to a *t*." I drummed my hands on the table before standing. The thought of getting my work done in time to watch some ESPN sounded amazing.

"Perfect. I'll get started," Tamara said as she made her way toward the pantry.

I nodded and pushed my hands through my hair before turning and heading out into the lobby. After jotting the numbers of the newly vacated rooms on a sticky note, I grabbed my cleaning buckets and took the stairs two at a time up to the second floor.

After I got to the first room, I slipped my earbuds in and cranked up my music. Through the familiarity of the songs and the monotony of cleaning, I felt my body relax. Whatever had stressed me out earlier felt like a distant memory. For now, I was just going to focus on getting my job done for the day.

I finished cleaning the rooms, put away all of the cleaning supplies, and started a load of laundry. By the time I was finished, Belle was up and puttering around in the kitchen. The pot roast was cooking in the oven, and the aroma made my mouth water.

I took a quick shower, and Tamara was making something in the stand mixer when I came back in. She had flour on her cheek, but her smile was wide when she caught my gaze. "I'm making rolls," she said over the sound of the mixer.

"Really?" I asked as I reached down and picked up Belle. I hooked my arm under her bum like a chair, and she hugged my neck, placing a big, big kiss on my cheek.

Tamara's cheeks flushed as she nodded. "It's been a long time since I've baked." She blew out her breath as her lips tipped up into a smile. "It feels good to have my hands in some dough again."

A genuine smile crept across my face. I'd spent so much of the week frowning that it felt good to work those muscles in the opposite direction. "I'm happy for you, T."

My nickname for Tamara came out so instinctively that I almost didn't catch it. But Tamara did. Her smile faltered as she stared at me. Then it reappeared, shyer this time. "Thanks, Miles."

I nodded, not sure how to address what just happened. From her smile, she was touched, and after our conversation earlier, I feared she thought it meant more than it did. But I couldn't just tell her to ignore it, that it was an old habit. Those explanations would just end up making me look like a jerk. So I decided the best thing to do was to pretend that it never happened.

I pulled Belle close to my chest as I glanced down at her. "Wanna go outside for some air?"

She giggled and nodded.

I didn't look back as I headed across the kitchen and out the back door. The cool night air hit me and I took in a deep breath. The sun had descended behind the trees, turning the sky above them a deep purple.

I set Belle down in the grass, and she moved around picking up sticks. I followed after her. I felt my mind empty as I watched her explore. I wasn't ready to think about Tamara. I wasn't ready to think about Shelby. I just wanted my life to be normal. Was that too much to ask?

"Up."

I startled and glanced down to see that Belle was

standing next to me with her arms pushed up to the sky. Her gaze was earnest as she studied me.

"Up," she repeated.

I picked her up and tucked my arm once again under her bum before I nuzzled her cheek. "You're the only uncomplicated woman in my life," I said as I pulled back to meet her wide eyes.

She giggled and then placed her hands on each of my cheeks. I started humming and her eyes widened. I grabbed onto one of her tiny hands and started moving around the yard. Her laugh spurred me on, and soon I was spinning her around and around, singing Disney songs at the top of my lungs.

She tipped her head back, laughing. My singing was turning breathless from exertion, and I slowed to catch my breath. A figure in the shadows caught my gaze. I stilled as realization hit me like a freight train. Shelby was standing there, her gaze trained on me and Belle.

My entire body froze and my heart felt like it was going to pound out of my chest. My soul sang as I took in the way her gaze was focused on me. There was something in her eyes that for a split second made me hope she regretted what she said to me last time she was here.

"'Elby," Belle said, snapping me out of my reverie. I glanced down to see Belle looking between Shelby and me. Her little eyebrows were drawn together like she was confused by what was happening. Not wanting her to worry, I kept my smile as I made my way over to Shelby.

"Hey, Belle," she said as the corners of her lips tipped up into a smile. Belle wiggled against my arm and Shelby reached out to grab her. They hugged and my heart bled at the sight. The two had a bond, and it made me so proud that my daughter felt connected to the woman I loved.

Finally, Shelby broke away from Belle. She glanced over at me before shifting her weight and giving me an unsure smile. "Hey."

"Hey."

Silence.

Belle seemed to grow bored and began to squirm against Shelby's arms. So Shelby set her down, and Belle wandered over to pick some flowers. I thought about telling her to leave the bush alone, but I needed all of my faculties about me. So I pushed my hand through my hair as I met Shelby's gaze once more.

"I've missed you." The words tumbled out of my mouth before I could stop them.

Shelby's eyes widened before she glanced around. "Oh."

I closed my eyes for a split second, cursing myself for saying those words. What was wrong with me? I'd poured my heart out to this woman, and she'd still walked away. I was holding onto the hope that we could be something, but with the way she was standing there, looking reserved, I feared she'd given up on us a while ago.

"Do me the honor of a dance?" Desperate to make this encounter less awkward, I did the first thing that came to mind. I reached out and grasped her hand. The warmth of her fingers and the softness of her skin sent jolts of electricity up my arm.

It was taking all of my strength not to pull her to my chest and never let her go.

At first, she was hesitant, but she didn't pull away. I took that as an opportunity, so I pulled her hand toward me as I stepped closer. My other hand found her waist, and I pressed gently with my palm, causing her to step close to me.

Everything about her. The warmth of her skin under her shirt. The smell of her hair. The familiarity of her perfume. Everything was slamming into me in waves, causing my heart to pound and my entire body to gravitate toward her. She was the only person in existence that I was meant to hold.

She was everything I wanted, and I wanted so desperately to tell her that without scaring her off. I just wasn't sure how.

"Miles, I..." Her voice was so soft that I almost couldn't hear it.

I pulled her in closer, wrapping my fingers around her hand and holding it to my chest. I closed my eyes as I pressed my cheek to the top of her head. "Just let me hold you for this moment," I whispered. I was begging, but I didn't care. I needed this woman like I needed air.

I knew, any second now, she was going to pull away,

leaving me cold and alone. So if she was willing to let me hold her, I was going to for as long as I could.

"Hey, Miles, you're out of butt...er..."

Shelby's entire body went stiff and she stopped moving. We both turned to see a very flustered Tamara standing on the porch with a dish towel in one hand and an empty box of butter in the other. Flour was still dusted across her cheeks. Her eyes were wide as she stared at Shelby and me.

Shelby jumped away as if she'd been poked with a hot iron. Her skin was pale as she shook her head. "I'm so sorry," she whispered before turning and heading over to the cottage.

I stared at her retreating frame before glancing over to Tamara, who had on an expression that I couldn't really read. I waved my hand toward the kitchen. "I'll get some out of the freezer in the garage. Watch Belle for a minute."

I didn't wait for Tamara to speak, instead, I hurried to the cottage after Shelby.

The light was on in the bedroom, and I walked in to find Shelby pulling clothes out of the closet. She looked panicked, and the memory of the night she'd left ten years ago slammed into me.

"What are you doing?" I asked as I neared her. I wanted to wrap my arms around her and pull her to my chest. I'd let this woman run away before, and I'd be damned if I was going to let her leave again.

"I'm looking for something," she said but didn't stop

moving. Almost all of the clothes in her closet were now draped on the bed.

"What?"

She paused. "A dress."

"For what?"

She glanced over at me before she disappeared into the closet once more. When she emerged she held a black dress. "I'm leaving for the weekend," she said as she set the dress down on the bed and headed back into the closet.

"Where are you going?" Desperation was starting to set in. I hated it, but I feared the longer we spent apart, the further she would pull away from me. I wasn't ready to let her go.

She rose up onto her tiptoes and started to pull down shoe boxes from the top of the closet. She looked over her shoulder at me. "I'm going to a wedding."

"A wedding?"

Her hand settled on a box, and as she pulled it down, a book tumbled out with it. She jumped out of the way to keep it from falling on her, and my gaze followed it as it thudded to the ground. Shelby hesitated before she bent down and picked it up. "What is this?"

I wasn't sure if she was asking me or if she was asking herself. It was strange that she didn't know. After all, she was the only person who had lived in the cottage since Charlotte...

And then realization dawned on me. I stepped forward to stop her, but she'd already flipped open the floral cover. I watched as she raked her gaze down the paper and then glanced up at me.

"Gran?"

I swallowed before I nodded. I had meant to tell her that her grandmother had lived here once, but I'd never gotten the chance. "Yes," I whispered.

Her cheeks flushed as she turned her attention to the book. "Wait. Why is this here?"

I sighed as I moved to collapse in the armchair a few feet away. "She lived here before you."

Shelby's body stiffened once more as she moved her gaze to meet mine. "What?"

I leaned forward, resting my elbows on my knees as my shoulders slumped. "This was her house. She had it built once she couldn't do stairs anymore."

Shelby was staring at me now. "Why didn't you tell me?"

I met her gaze head-on. "Would you have stayed?"

She studied me for what felt like an eternity. Then she sighed, set the journal on the box of shoes, and grabbed the dress. "I should have never come back here," she muttered under her breath as she turned and headed to the front door.

Anger pricked at the back of my neck. I was so emotionally drained that my ability to filter my thoughts was waning. "What does that mean?" I asked as I strode after her.

She was at her car now, shoving her stuff onto the

backseat. "I should have never come back here," she said, this time louder.

I was standing next to the car, the urge to beg her to stay contrasted against my desire to tell her to leave. I didn't want my heart to break again, and I was scared that in a matter of seconds, she was going to pull it out of my chest and leave it bleeding on the ground.

"Then why did you?"

She paused before she slammed the door and turned to face me. Her gaze was so dark, I couldn't read what she was feeling. "You're right, I shouldn't have ever trusted you or my grandmother. My life was simpler in New York."

"Then why don't you go back?" The words tasted bitter on my tongue. I knew I needed to stop. If I wasn't careful, she would leave forever.

But I was tired of hurting. I needed a reprieve. And maybe if she hated me, I could finally stop loving her as much as I did.

She stopped to look at me. "Maybe I should."

Her words were like a knife to my gut. I was a fish on the ground, desperate to breathe but slowly succumbing to the inevitability of my death.

"I'm not going to stop you," I said, emotions taking over and causing my voice to deepen as I stared at her.

"I don't want you to stop me."

I blinked, the harshness of her words washing over me. "Then I won't."

For a split second, I thought I saw tears brimming her eyes. My heart ached to comfort her. To pull her into my arms and admit that everything I'd just said was a lie. To beg her to stay. To vow that I would always love and protect her.

I was that person for her. I'd been the one to collect all of her broken pieces. I was her protector. How could I turn away from her now? My throat tightened, and it hurt to swallow. But I stood my ground. I needed her to reach out as well. I couldn't always be one who was vulnerable. At some point, she was going to have to do the same for me.

"Goodbye, Miles." She studied me before she grabbed the car door handle and pulled. Dinging from inside the car filled the silence between us.

I stared at her, daring her to leave. Daring her to make this the last time we spoke. Despite my desire to stay with her, I took a step back to see what she would do.

"Goodbye, Shelby." The words left my lips, fading into the darkness that now surrounded us. My breath hitched in my chest as I waited for her to make her move.

She stared off into the distance before she slipped into the driver's seat and slammed the door. The sound of her tires spinning on the gravel echoed in my mind as I watched her peel away from me. Away from the inn. Away from everything that had brought us together.

I watched her taillights grow smaller, but then I

dropped my gaze. I'd watched her drive away once. I wasn't going to do it again.

I was going to be the one to disappear first.

I hurried across the yard and up the back porch. I pulled open the door and walked into the kitchen. Tamara had some music on and was dancing around the kitchen, much to Belle's delight. When she saw me, she stopped.

"What's wrong?"

All I could do was stand there. My body felt numb as my mind swam with thoughts. I couldn't process what had happened, and yet I could feel the finality of Shelby's departure. I closed my eyes for a moment before I spoke. "Shelby and I are officially...done."

10

SHELBY

SWEET TEA &
SOUTHERN GENTLEMAN

I LET OUT a sob as I slowed to a stop. The light in front of me was yellow, and I had the chance to speed through, but I didn't want to. My tears were blurring the road, and I needed a moment to sob into my hands before I drove the rest of the way to Abigail's.

So much had happened in such a short amount of time, and my brain hadn't been able to process any of it. All I knew was that I wanted to turn around. I wanted to go back to the inn. Back to Miles' arms. I wanted him to tell me that I was safe.

My shoulders shook as I wept into my hands. This wasn't how I'd wanted any of this to go. I'd wanted to pull up to the inn and see Miles standing there. I'd wanted him to pull me into his arms and tell me to never leave.

And at first, I'd thought that was a possibility. Especially when I saw him dancing in the yard with Belle. My heart surged when he saw me and started to walk over. And when his hands found my waist and he pulled me close, I knew I was home.

Then there was Tamara. She looked like the picture-perfect wife with the mixing bowl in her hands and the flour dusted across her cheek. The way her countenance shone when she laid eyes on Miles, I would be a fool not to see that something could happen between them.

Then, as if adding salt to my wound, there was the journal. And the fact that Miles had lied to me about the cottage. I wasn't ready for so many wounds to be open at once.

Fear had taken hold of me, and all I could do was run.

It was all I'd ever been good at.

The shrill noise of the horn behind me pulled me from my thoughts. I whipped my gaze up to see the man behind me flick his hand at me. I raised my hand in apology as I grasped the steering wheel and pressed on the gas.

Thankfully, I made it to Abigail's in one piece. The entire drive was a blur, so I was grateful when I pulled into an empty parking spot and turned off the car. I grabbed my purse, my dress, and my grandmother's journal before slamming the door behind me and hurrying up the back staircase.

I had to shift all of my belongings to one arm so I could dig around in my purse for the spare key Abigail had given me. I let out a breath of relief when I found the cool metal and shoved the key into the lock. Just as I turned the handle, I heard voices laughing inside.

Not wanting to interrupt Abigail and whomever she had over, I slipped through the door and shut it quietly behind me. I blew my hair from my face as I engaged the lock. The kitchen was empty, which meant I would have a clear shot to Abigail's bedroom without being seen.

The two voices were coming from the living room. One was Abigail's, and the other was a man's voice, low and smooth.

Curiosity won out, and as I reached the corner of the kitchen, I peered around it. Abigail was sitting on the couch. She was laying her head on the shoulder of a very broad, blond-haired man. It must be Anders. She had told me that he was back and she'd been waiting in a break in his schedule to plan some time together. Although, her excitement hadn't been at the level I'd expect for a girl in the first stages of a relationship.

But now, seeing how close they were to each other, maybe I'd been wrong.

"Shelby?" Abigail pushed up from where she was sitting before I could disappear. Her gaze landed on me, and within a matter of seconds, her brows furrowed as her gaze searched my face. "I'll be right back," she said to Anders as she hopped up and crossed the space between us.

By the time she got to me, the tears had started once

more. I'd managed to get myself together, but her look of concern broke the dam inside of me.

She wrapped her arm around my shoulders and ushered me into her bedroom. I collapsed on her bed, still clutching all of the items that I'd come in with.

"What happened?" she asked as she flopped down next to me.

I stared up at the ceiling, letting the tears flow from my eyes and into my hair that was spread out around me. "Miles and I are officially...done." I closed my eyes, hating that I was saying those words. I had hoped that we could work through things. That door was still open, even if it was only a sliver.

But I was too broken, too hurt, to have hope that we could make it work. I wasn't ready to face my past. He couldn't give up on the chance to make things work for his daughter. So we were at an impasse. The best thing I could do was walk away.

"He broke it off for good?" Abigail's asked.

I appreciated the snap of annoyance in her tone. I loved that she wanted to protect me. But I also didn't want her to think badly of Miles. I shook my head. "I broke it off."

She stilled. "Why?"

I sighed as I closed my eyes and covered them with my elbow. I shrugged. "It was just never going to work. There's so much in our past that I fear we can never move forward. And I've spent so much of my life stuck in the past, that the kindest thing for both of us is to call it like it is and walk away."

Silence. "Are you sure that's what you want?"

I nodded as I pushed myself up and wrapped my arm around my knees, drawing them to my chest. "I have no other option."

Abigail's gaze was sympathetic as she studied my face. "Well, you know that I'm here for you. And you can stay as long as you want."

I forced a smile. "Thanks." I took in a deep breath as my gaze drifted over to the bedroom door. "Anders back?"

She nodded. "Yeah."

I was happy at least one of us had a functioning romantic life. "That must be nice."

A strange expression passed over her face, but it only lasted for a moment before it was gone. I thought about asking her what that meant, but I decided to just leave it. I knew that she was stressed about her sister and worried about leaving her to go on dates with Anders. So I could only assume that's what it had to be.

She smiled and nodded. "I'm excited.

I eyed her, noting that there was definitely a lack of enthusiasm in her voice. "Really?"

She glowered at me even though she was still smiling. "Really."

"Okay."

"Speaking of Anders, I should get back out there. He's going to think I like you more than I like him."

I nodded. "He would be right."

She laughed as she pulled open the bedroom door and then turned to study me. "Are you really going to be okay?"

My smile faltered, but I forced it back. "I'll be okay."

She eyed me before she nodded and slipped into the hallway, pulling the door closed behind her.

Now alone, I flopped back onto the bed. I turned to my side and curled up into a ball. Then I closed my eyes as I allowed my heart to slowly break.

It was a feeling I'd grown accustomed to. Like a toothache that wouldn't lessen. My life—my future—was always going to be an unhappy one.

The more I came to accept that instead of fight it, the more peace I would feel. I was never meant to find happiness.

It just wasn't in the cards for me.

———

THE NEXT MORNING went by in a blur. I was so busy packing and helping Abigail with Samuel that I didn't have time to cry or even think about Miles...more than ten times.

Truth was, he was the first thing I thought of when I went to sleep, and his face was the first thing I saw when I woke up in the next morning. And then, every so often after that, his face would float into my mind and I would have to use all of my energy to push it back out.

Today, it was easier to refocus my thoughts because I had a deadline. I needed to be at the airport at eleven for my flight at noon. I was excited and nervous to see Titan again. Excited to focus on something other than Harmony, my past, or Miles. Nervous because Titan was still a stranger to me. Even though he'd sent me some newsletter gossip columns about the two of us, I still didn't know the man.

And I was about to spend the weekend pretending that I knew him intimately.

"Ready?" Abigail asked as she rushed out of Samuel's room with him cradled to her shoulder.

I finished my mug of coffee and then nodded as I hopped off the barstool. "Yep. The ride share guy texted and said he'll be here in five minutes. "

"Good. I can make sure you get in and that you're safe, and then I have to head to the shop. Without you there, I'm going to be scrambling."

"I get it. No worries."

"You do know that if I could, I'd drop you off."

I shook my head. Abigail was too nice. "No, I wouldn't let you. The drive to the airport is three hours. There's no way you would have time to get back before you open."

Abigail studied me. "Still. I would do it if I could."

I gave her a quick hug and a squeeze. "I'll be fine. Don't forget that I lived in New York City, alone, for the last ten years. I think I can make it to the airport in one piece."

She studied me and then nodded. Samuel squirmed and made some grunting noise. "Where is your mother?" Abigail sighed under her breath as she hurried over to Sabrina's door and gave it a few good knocks.

My phone chimed, and I didn't have to look to know it was my ride. I slung my purse on my shoulder and gave Abigail a big smile. "Well, I'm off. Hold the fort down for me while I'm gone."

Abigail bounced Samuel a few times as she continued to stand outside of Sabrina's room. "Be safe. Text me throughout the day so I can live vicariously through you."

We'd spent an evening, a few days ago, researching Titan, his family, and his ex. My eyes had almost fallen out of my head when I saw the gorgeous supermodel that he thought would be jealous if I came.

I was pretty sure I would look like a bridge troll next to her, but I'd made a commitment. Plus, I needed to get out of Harmony for a bit. So I was going to put on my big girl panties and pretend to be an NFL player's main squeeze.

"I'd walk down with you, but I think I'll need a bucket of water if I'm going to get Sabrina up."

I waved away her words. "I'll be fine. I'll call you while I'm in the car so he knows that people know where I am and are expecting me at the airport." I pointed a finger in her direction. "Don't be surprised if I call you honey or babe."

She gave me a two-finger salute. "I would expect nothing less."

I laughed and she grinned. Then I gave her one final wave and headed out of the apartment. Once I was in the car and driving toward the airport, I finally let out my breath. I was going to have a reprieve for a few days, and I was looking forward to it.

Part of me hoped that by the time I got back, Miles would be a distant memory and he and Tamara would be engaged and setting a date. That way, I could start the process of finding acceptance and happiness for them.

But I knew that was a fantasy.

I could forget my problems for a moment, but I would end up right back where I'd started.

Brokenhearted and alone.

11

MILES

SWEET TEA &
SOUTHERN GENTLEMAN

I FELT a sort of peace when I woke up the next morning and got into the shower. Even though I had a huge, gaping hole in my heart, knowing that Shelby wasn't going to make her way back to the inn helped calm me down. I wasn't constantly looking out the window at every sound, wondering if it was Shelby driving back to the inn.

In a way, I could close the door on her. And that was going to help me move forward, even if I wasn't quite ready to accept where my future was going.

I wrapped a towel around my waist as I stepped out onto the bathroom mat. I swiped at the fogged mirror, creating water droplets in the process. I stared at my reflection for a second before I sighed and placed my fists on the counter and pushed down. I was frustrated with how things ended with Shelby yesterday. And even though all I wanted to do was drive after her, I knew that wasn't the answer to my problems.

Shelby needed time and space. I couldn't force her into talking to me or having a relationship with me. All I could do was be here if she ever decided she wanted to come back sometime in the future. Regardless of me, Harmony Inn was still her home. It was her grandmother's legacy.

After I dressed, I headed out of my room and into the kitchen. Tamara had offered to let me sleep in after I came storming into the kitchen last night, following my interaction with Shelby. I'd been more than happy to take her up on her offer.

She was dancing around the kitchen with Belle, humming Disney princess songs, while the smell of waffles and coffee filled the air. I leaned against the doorframe as I watched Belle squeal with glee. I'd never seen my daughter take to someone as fast as she did to Tamara. Sure, she was her mother. But to Belle, Tamara was a stranger. Not anymore. They looked like two peas in a pod.

Tamara noticed me first. She stopped spinning and offered me a wide smile. Her cheeks were flushed, and she was out of breath. "Morning," she said as she set down Belle, who continued her own form of spinning.

"Morning," I said as I pushed off the wall and walked into the room.

"Did you sleep well?"

I shrugged. I wasn't ever going to sleep well with Shelby gone and my heart breaking, but I had mustered an adequate night's sleep. "It was nice to sleep in, that's for sure," I said as I turned and gave her a wide smile.

She gave me a shy smile in response and then perked up. "I made us a picnic lunch. I was thinking after we finish things here and Belle wakes up from her nap, we could go on a little beach excursion." She shrugged and looked nervously up at me. "How does that sound?"

I glanced over at Belle, who was now drawing on the whiteboard on the wall. I didn't want to go. I wanted to wallow in my self-pity. But I knew Belle would love it, so I nodded. "Sounds like something we need."

Tamara looked relieved as she blew out her breath. "Oh, good." Then she motioned toward the beeping waffle iron. "I'll finish up here and then feed Belle, if you want to get started on cleaning the rooms."

I studied her. I hadn't realized until now how smooth the operation of the inn had become. Tamara had really changed. She was more present. More attentive. Happier. This was the kind of life I'd imagined us living when we first got together.

I liked how it felt to not be alone. To have someone in my life who had similar goals and aspirations. Who helped carry the load of the inn and parenthood. The ease of having someone else around who was reaching for the same goal as I was tempted me.

"Uh, thanks," I said, startled at my own thoughts. I

didn't like them. I liked the sharing of responsibility that came with having Tamara around...but I wasn't in love with Tamara.

I'd thought about it last night as I lay in bed, going over what had happened with Shelby and how broken our relationship was. I tried to imagine an intimate relationship with Tamara where we shared our life and our bed ...but the desire just wasn't there. No matter how much I wanted to forget Shelby, I couldn't

I loved her. I always had and always would.

And I wasn't sure if I could subject Tamara to a loveless relationship. I deserved happiness and love, and so did she.

I planted a kiss on the top of Belle's head, grabbed a cooling waffle, and headed out to the receptionist desk, where I glanced over what needed to be done for the day. I had the gardener coming to clean up and trim the lawn. I had two guests leaving. I had some rooms to tidy up—business was really booming around here—and I needed to clean the living room in a bad way.

After making my list, I headed to the supply closet, shoved the last bits of my waffle into my mouth, and got started.

Tamara handled breakfast, and soon, the noise level in the inn decreased to almost nothing. We were hosting a lot of the construction workers, and they were loud when they were around, which contrasted against the hum of families and older couples who normally frequented the inn.

I wasn't going to complain, though. They kept the lights on and money rolling in. For once, I didn't have to worry about how I was going to pay the mortgage. I knew that I had what I needed in the bank.

I didn't finish my jobs until well after one. After I vacuumed and dusted the living room, I wiped everything down and then returned all of my cleaning supplies to the closet, taking a mental note to stop by Godwin's in the next few days to pick up supplies.

Tamara was sitting on the back deck with a hot mug of tea and her feet up on the railing when I finished. I allowed the back door to swing shut as I walked out to join her.

She held her finger to her lips as she giggled. "Shh. Belle's asleep."

I gave her a sheepish smile and sat down on an adjacent chair. "Ah." I leaned back, letting all of my muscles relax as I sunk into the chair. "Did she go down easy?"

Tamara's eyes were wide as she shook her head. "Not today. She was a busy girl."

My heart surged at the mention of my daughter. It was taking all of my strength not to hurry to her room and give her a big squeeze. She was so sassy and cute, and when I wasn't around her, I missed her. "She's turning into such a stinker."

Tamara nodded as she turned her attention to the

woods that surrounded the inn. Then her gaze drifted to the cottage and her expression stilled. I knew what she was going to ask me before she even said the words.

"I haven't heard from her," I said, beating her to any questions she might have.

Tamara glanced over at me as she wrapped her arms around her chest. She watched me for a second before she sighed. "I don't know how to say this..." she said slowly.

I frowned. "Say what?"

She flicked her gaze over to me a few times. I could see the turmoil inside of her.

"Just tell me," I said, panic rising in my chest. What was she going to say?

"I was just on social media and..." She reached down and flipped over her phone, which had been sitting face-down on her lap. "I swear, I didn't go looking, it just came up on my feed." She turned the screen on and scrolled a few times before she handed me her phone.

At first, I didn't understand what I was looking at. But the familiar light brown hair and dark eyes of Shelby registered in my brain, and my entire body felt like it was on fire. She was standing in front of an airport with her arms wrapped around a very large man. Her head was tipped back with her hair swirling around her and she was laughing. The man had his two arms wrapped around her waist and he was holding her close.

Too close.

My mouth went dry, and no matter how many times I swallowed, it didn't help. I was angry. Hurt. Betrayed.

Who was this man? I scrolled to the bottom of the photo.

Linebacker, Titan Strom, hugging mystery girl who has the world questioning, has the NFL's playboy finally settled down?

I cursed under my breath. This was her trip this weekend? She was flitting off to some small Vermont town to... what? Date another guy? I tossed Tamara's phone into her lap and shrugged. "She said she wanted to move on. I guess she got a jump on it."

Tamara studied me. I could tell that she didn't believe me. I wanted her to think that I didn't care, but she knew as well as I did that I cared.

A lot.

"I don't..." Tamara stopped talking and pinched her lips as she stared at me.

I could tell she had more she wanted to say. I wasn't sure I was ready to hear it, but I knew I couldn't sit here in silence while she held in it. I needed her to say it before I went insane. "What?" I asked, my voice coming out gruffer than I intended.

The sound wasn't lost on Tamara. Her eyes were wide as she studied me. "It's probably nothing."

I shook my head. I didn't need her to sugarcoat this. I needed her to rip off the bandage. "Tell me."

She sighed, picked up her phone, and started scrolling

once more. "When I saw that, I wanted to see if this was something new or if they had a history." Her cheeks turned pink. "Not to dig up dirt...I was just curious because I thought she really cared about you."

"Tamara," I said, my tone turning to one of warning. I wasn't sure if I could handle what she was about to say.

Her eyes were wide as she studied me but then she returned to her phone screen before handing it over to me. "These were taken a few weeks ago. She was with Titan at some coffee shop in New York."

I took her phone and held it in my hand for a moment. I didn't want to look down. I didn't want to think there was a chance she'd been thinking about another man when she was with me.

I couldn't just sit here, holding Tamara's phone hostage. I glanced down, making sure that the first thing I looked at was the date. My heart sank. It was the weekend before the will reading. My stomach soured as I stared at Shelby's smile and the way Titan had his arm wrapped around her shoulders. He was leaning a little too close for my liking, and Shelby didn't look like she disliked what was happening. She looked...content.

I tossed Tamara's phone into her lap once more and stood up. Rage pulsed through my body as I stood in front of the railing and stared angrily at the scene in front of me. What had started out as a calm interaction between Tamara and me, had turned into a wake-up call.

Shelby and I were really done. We were over. She

kept telling me, but I refused to listen. Instead, I'd believed in my love so much that I thought—stupidly— that it would bleed over to her and she would feel something for me too. Even if it wasn't the soul burning love I felt for her.

"I'm sure it's nothing, Miles." Tamara's voice was soft and cautious.

I chuckled, hating that I'd been such an idiot about Shelby for so long. "No, it's fine. You did the right thing telling me." I pushed my hands through my hair, my shoulders sagging with defeat. "It's better that I know now. Then, when she comes back with a ring on her finger, I'm prepared." I looked over my shoulder and gave Tamara a weak smile.

She studied me and then nodded. "I just wanted to protect you."

"I know."

Silence engulfed us as we lingered on the deck. I wasn't sure what to say, and Tamara looked the same. I glanced toward the inn and sighed. "You wanted to go to the beach?" I asked.

Tamara gave me a hopeful smile. "I packed a lunch. Belle and I were waiting for you to finish." She glanced down at her watch. "She's been asleep for an hour and a half. It's probably time for her to get up." Tamara stood up, the chair rocking back and forth from the movement. "If we're going to go, we should go now before it gets too dark."

I nodded and held the door open so she could walk inside. "Sounds good. I'll go get our daughter up."

Tamara was halfway to the fridge, but she stopped and turned around. Her eyes were wide, and I could tell my words were lingering in her mind like they were lingering in mine.

Our daughter.

Two little words that meant nothing on their own, but together they held a meaning that was deeper than I was ready to face. So I just gave her a weak smile and then ducked my head and zeroed in on Belle's room, hoping that when I got back she'd forget I said anything.

12

ABIGAIL

SWEET TEA &
SOUTHERN GENTLEMAN

I WAS EXHAUSTED. My entire body ached when I climbed into my car after finishing up at the shop. When Fanny walked in to take over, I'd nearly cried. I hadn't realized how much help Shelby had been, and I wasn't sure what I was going to do if she ever decided to leave.

It wasn't like the town was crawling with people who wanted to work for me. In the past, doing it all myself had worked. But with the increase in foot traffic and having to take care of Samuel, I was feeling the pinch.

I kicked off my shoes as soon as I got into my apartment. Sabrina was in her room and Samuel was with her, which made me smile. I felt hopeful that things were getting better for her. I was seeing more initiation on her part, which helped lessen the stress I felt when I was gone. I was constantly trying to keep up with demand at the shop while worrying about what was going on back home.

If she could handle the home stress, it would be a load off of my shoulders.

"I'm back," I called toward Sabrina's door.

I heard something drop followed by an "umph" before Sabrina appeared in the doorway. "Hey," she said. Her cheeks were flushed and her hair was pulled up into a messy bun. She was wearing a t-shirt and sweatpants, and looked more alive than I'd seen her look since Samuel's birth.

"Hey," I replied, giving her a wide smile. It felt good to see a glimmer of the old Sabrina. For the first time, it felt as if the sun were shining again. Maybe, just maybe, we were coming out of the storm. "How did it go here?"

Sabrina glanced behind her and then back to me. "Good. Samuel and I are going through my old clothes and getting rid of stuff that doesn't fit." She disappeared only to reappear with Samuel in her arms. She nuzzled his cheek and he stared up at her and smiled.

I missed my nephew, so I set my purse down and crossed the room. "I wanna see him," I said as I took him from her arms and gave him my own snuggle.

Sabrina studied him for a moment before glancing over at me. "How was the shop?"

I sighed, not wanting to talk about it. I had to convince myself over and over again that I needed the shop and liked the shop. But when the tiny bookstore-slash-coffee shop was overrun by cranky, caffeine-deprived construction workers, it was the last place I wanted to be.

I yawned and made my way into the kitchen, looking for the chocolate I'd bought a few days ago. After setting Samuel down in his bouncer, I began to pull open the cupboards. "Something is going on. I've never seen this town so packed with people. I thought it was for those condos they are putting along the beach, but now I'm thinking there's something more." When I came up empty-handed, I glanced over at Sabrina. "Did you eat my chocolate?"

She was leaning against the doorframe, watching me. When my question registered, her eyes widened as she pulled back. "I, um...er."

I shook my head. I'd let her eat all the chocolate in Harmony if that meant my sister was finally coming back to me. "It's fine. I can get some another time. Besides"—I motioned to my hips—"I've been eating all the baked goods at the shop. It's not like I'm in need of sugar or anything like that."

Sabrina chuckled. "So, what are your plans for tonight?"

I pushed my hands through my hair and pulled it up into a bun on the top of my head. I hadn't really thought about it. After all, I'd figured I'd come home and have auntie duty. With Sabrina up and awake, I just might have a shot at a night out.

"I, um..." I glanced around, enjoying how carefree I felt. "I'll probably text Anders to see if he wants to do dinner."

Sabrina nodded just as Samuel began to fuss. She crossed the room and scooped him back up. "I think we'll finish the laundry, then eat, and then take a bath." She bounced him a few times. "And then early bedtime."

I scrunched up my nose. "Actually, those plans sound much better than mine. Maybe I'll stick around—"

"Nope. You're young and single. You need to get out and get a life." She raised her finger and waggled it in my direction.

I couldn't stop the smile that spread across my lips. My big sister was back, and it felt amazing. Even though I really did want to stay and veg out on the couch, I loved that she was aware enough to care that I get out.

I settled on an apple from the bowl on the counter even though it wasn't chocolate. I took a big bite and passed by my sister as I headed into my room. "I've gotta get dressed up if I'm going to woo anyone," I said over my shoulder.

"Fashion show?" Sabrina called back.

After modeling five different outfits, we settled on a simple black dress and flats. Something that looked like I'd dressed up, but I wasn't trying too hard. I pulled my hair back with a banana clip, which allowed strands of hair to fall forward to frame my face.

I shot Anders a text, and he responded with a curt, "Get over here now."

I giggled as I sent a salute emoji and then turned back

to Sabrina. She was watching me with a soft smile on her lips. "He really makes you that happy?" she asked.

Her question took me off guard as I slipped my phone into my purse. I wasn't quite sure how to answer that. Things with Anders were so new, and I wasn't sure if I *liked* him liked him or just liked the idea of not being alone anymore.

I'd felt so lost before Shelby and Anders came into my life. I was just grateful that I had people to hang out with. Friends who made me laugh. I'd spent so much time since moving here just trying to figure out who I was that I'd lost a piece of myself.

I finally felt like I was getting that back, and it was...amazing.

"He makes me feel...normal again."

Sabrina studied me before she nodded. "I'm happy for you, Abi."

There was a sad sort of tone to her voice. But then she gave me a smile and turned to head back into her room. Feeling selfish, I decided to let her reaction go for now. Tonight, I just wanted to be happy. I wanted to pretend that everything was back to normal and that we were all moving forward. Sabrina, Samuel, and I. That what happened with Trevor was done and Sabrina was ready to face motherhood and the future.

I wasn't going to make her do it on her own, but I also wasn't going to carry her water for her. She was strong, and I would be there to pick up the pieces when she wasn't.

I pulled out some lipstick and applied it before I grabbed my keys and purse, and then hurried from the apartment. I was ready for some time alone with Anders. I was ready to feel like a woman again. And I was ready to ignore my responsibilities until tomorrow.

IT TOOK Anders a few seconds longer than I'd expected to come to the door when I knocked. I stood outside of his apartment, bouncing up and down on the balls of my feet, waiting for him to come get me. When he pulled open the door, I had to take a step back. His hair was disheveled, and he had a beer and a game controller in one hand.

His eyes widened when he saw me, and suddenly his free hand was around my waist and pulling me close. "You look amazing," he slurred into my neck.

I wrinkled my nose as I pulled back a bit. "Are you okay?" I asked, not really wanting to be here if he was drunk. But I didn't want to go home. This was my break, and I wanted it to last as long as I could make it.

He pressed his lips to mine before pulling back. "Now that you're here, I'm good." He grasped my hand and pulled me into the apartment.

I managed to kick off my shoes by the door as he kept ahold of me and led me down the hallway and into his room. He jumped onto his bed and resumed his game. I lingered next to him for a moment before I climbed up next to him.

This wasn't how I'd seen our evening going, but I didn't want to go back to my apartment and I didn't want to be alone. So I grabbed a nearby pillow and curled up with it. My mind wandered as I watched Anders' character on the screen. He was going through some castle ruins looking for men to kill.

Anders was definitely animated when he played. He shook the bed when he got shot at and yelled at the screen when he was shooting his gun.

I yawned and glanced around, wondering if he was ever going to pay attention to me. From his text, I'd thought he wanted me to come over. But now that I was here, it was like I was invisible.

I realized that it was going to be a while before Anders was ready to pay attention to me, so I slipped off his bed and made my way to the door. "I'm going to get something to drink," I said. But if Anders heard, he didn't move to acknowledge me. He just continued to shout at the TV screen.

I sighed as I made my way down the hallway and into the kitchen. I closed my eyes for a moment, taking in a deep breath and reveling in the silence that surrounded me.

My muscles relaxed and the tension in my body lessened, so I opened my eyes and glanced around. I needed something warm to drink.

After combing the cupboards, I found some herbal tea. I didn't want to drink coffee because I still needed to sleep, so this would do the trick.

I found a pot, filled it with water, and set it on the stove. While it warmed, I started searching the kitchen for a mug. I finally found one, way up on the top shelf. I sighed as I stared at it. Maybe if I rose up on my tiptoes I could touch the handle with the tips of my fingers.

My fingers brushed the shelf, but no matter how hard I strained, I couldn't quite get them on the mug's handle. I closed my eyes and reached harder, until suddenly, I felt warm skin brush my exposed shoulder. I ripped open my eyes to see an arm next to mine as it reached for the mug and grabbed ahold of it.

Relief filled my chest as I glanced over my shoulder expecting to see Anders, but instead, I was met with the dark eyes and dark, damp hair of Bash. He was standing centimeters away from me with a towel wrapped around his waist and nothing else.

"You looked like you needed some help," he said as he dropped the mug into my hand and then took a step back. His gaze was dark and unreadable as he stared at me.

My lips parted, but no noise came out. I swallowed as my gaze drifted down to the tattoos he had across his chest that were broken up by large, jagged scars. My skin pricked with heat as I took in his muscles and the last droplets of water that hadn't dried yet.

Could he hear my pounding heart?

He cleared his throat, drawing my attention up. His gaze met mine for a moment longer before he turned and disappeared down the hall and into his room.

I stood there, frozen to my spot, staring at the mug that Bash had placed in my hand. My entire body warmed when the memory of his chest brushing against my skin replayed in my head over and over and over again.

Did he feel something too?

I closed my eyes. I could still see the soulful look in his gaze as he stared down at me. I could feel his intensity as he studied me. Goosebumps flooded my body, and I allowed myself to sit with my feelings for a moment longer before I shifted my weight and blinked a few times, snapping myself back to reality.

I turned and set the mug down. I placed both hands on the counter and stared at the stained laminate. I felt stupid. Had I just imagined this all?

I covered my face with my hands. What was wrong with me?

I'd needed a mug. Bash saw I couldn't reach. He got one down for me.

Here I was, acting like an idiot, thinking that he was professing his love for me. He was coming out of the bathroom, saw me struggling, and helped. I laughed into my hands. I was so grateful that I hadn't said anything and that no one else had been around to see my reaction.

"There's something wrong with you, Abigail," I whispered under my breath. I needed to have my head checked or something. Or I just needed Anders to put the dumb controller down and pay attention to me.

I filled my mug with the boiling hot water and then dunked the tea bag a few times. I grabbed a nearby paper towel and wrapped it around the mug so my hand wouldn't burn, then I hurried into Anders' room.

He was still sitting on his bed, staring at the screen in front of him. I settled back down on the spot I'd vacated earlier, brought the mug to my lips, and gingerly took a sip.

I allowed my gaze to drift over to Bash's closed door once, before I forced it back to the TV and vowed I wouldn't allow my imagination to run wild anymore. Bash was just a nice guy who was helping out his roommate's girlfriend. He kept an eye on me while Anders was away, and now that Anders was back, I wasn't going to see much of him anymore.

I needed to remember that. I needed to focus on what I did have—even if that guy wasn't paying any attention to me. He was the one I was seeing. He was the one that wanted me.

MY ENTIRE BODY lurched as I startled awake. My heart pounded in my chest as I glanced around, trying to get my bearings. A soft glow filled the room from Anders' TV, but he was no longer playing. He was passed out on his bed with a controller in one hand and a beer in the other.

I pushed myself up to sitting as I took in a deep breath. What time was it and when had I fallen asleep? I glanced around the room. What a disaster of a night.

I thought I was coming over here to spend time with Anders. Apparently, spending time together meant me sitting next to him while he played video games.

I had gotten more attention from Sabrina today than I got from Anders this whole night. I sighed as I swung my legs over the side of the bed and stood. I pressed my hands into my lower back as the tension in my body began to dissipate.

Then I proceeded to turn off Anders TV, take his controller and beer bottle from him, and pull his blanket over his body so he wouldn't be cold. I gathered my mug of ice-cold tea and slipped out of his room, shutting his door behind me.

I tiptoed through the hallway, allowing myself to wonder for a moment if Bash were asleep or awake on the other side of the wall...before I shook my head and forced those thoughts from my mind before they became a permeant fixture in my head.

I moved to slip into the kitchen to deposit my mug into the sink and throw away Anders' bottle, but I was stopped short when I saw a large, dark figure leaning against the counter.

Bash.

Again.

He was dressed this time. He had on a worn cotton shirt and a pair of plaid pajama pants. His hair was dry and tousled in a way that made a woman want to run her fingers through it.

I let out a small "eep" before my cheeks heated and I felt like an idiot.

"Heading out?" Bash asked, his gaze drifting to my hands. When it focused on the beer bottle, his gaze darkened.

"This is Anders'," I said, faster than I meant to.

His gaze met mine, and before I could think, he crossed the room and took it from me. "I figured." He tossed it into the blue bin next to the sink. It must have hit other glass bottles because it made a tinkling noise when it fell.

"He's passed out on the bed. I turned everything off. Hopefully he gets some good sleep tonight," I said, glancing in the direction of Anders' room before looking back at Bash.

He'd returned to leaning against the counter. He picked up the mug that was sitting next to him, took a sip, and then set it back down.

"Do you need a ride?" He didn't look at me when he spoke. Instead, he stared at the ground in front of him.

"I'll be okay. I drove here." Then realization hit me. "I didn't drink, if that's what you're worried about."

He glanced up at me for a moment before he shook his

head. "I'm not worried about that. I just..." He paused, narrowing his eyes at me for a moment before letting out his breath. "It's my job as Anders' friend to make sure his girl gets home safe, that's all." He shoved his hands into the front pockets of his pajama pants and shrugged.

"Oh," was all I could say. I wanted to ask why he cared so much. I'd had boyfriends in the past. Their best friends could never be bothered to lift a finger to help me. Why was Bash so loyal?

He must have sensed my confusion because he pushed off the counter. He was now towering over me as he stared into my eyes. "We go way back. Anders saved me from a very dark place."

I couldn't help but stare up at him, mesmerized by how deep his gaze was. There was so much to this man, and I was only getting a glimpse. "What happened?" My voice was breathy but I didn't care. I wanted to know more about Bash. I wanted to figure him out.

He stared at me before his gaze drifted to my lips. My breath caught in my throat as I waited. But nothing ever came. Instead, he turned away from me. But in the process, he knocked the mug I was holding from my hand, spilling the ice-cold tea all over my dress.

I yelped and jumped back. I hadn't noticed that Bash was standing on the hem of my dress, and suddenly, the front seam of my dress was ripped apart. I stood there, shocked by the way Bash had looked at me mixed with the cool breeze I could now feel.

Bash looked horrified as he stared at me and my dress. Before I could blink, he had his shirt off and was handing it to me. "I'm so sorry," he muttered.

I shook my head. "It's okay," I whispered. I held his shirt, not sure what to do with it. I was still covered in tea and I didn't want it to get wet.

"It's okay. I don't need it back," he said, motioning toward the shirt.

I knew I shouldn't notice, but I couldn't help but watch the ripple of his muscles across his arm and chest as he moved. His scars and tattoos were still there. A history that I wanted to know more about.

I wanted to ask him. But I wasn't sure how to ask any of the questions that slammed through my mind.

"Come with me." Suddenly, his hand was in my mine. His warm calloused fingers sent electricity throughout my whole body.

I was too stunned to protest. So I allowed him to guide me through the hallway and into his room. I stood in the center, trying to keep my gaze focused on the wall, instead of letting curiosity get the better of me. What he had in his room would surely tell me something about who he was.

The sound of a dresser drawer shutting drew my attention over. Bash had pulled out a pair of basketball shorts and laid them on his bed. Then he pushed his door halfway closed and grabbed a towel that was hanging on the back of the door.

"Here," he said as he set it down on the bed next to the

shorts. "Change and then come out." He lingered in the doorway for a moment before he brought his gaze up to meet mine.

All I could do was nod.

Once he was gone, I slipped out of the dress, dried off, and then dressed in his basketball shorts and shirt. I felt better...warmer.

I allowed my gaze to drift around the room, but I didn't come up with anything. His decorations were nonexistent. He had only a few things on his dresser next to his TV. If I thought I was going to learn who this man was through his room...I was wrong.

Frustrated, I moved back out to the hallway.

Bash was standing next to his door, looking like he'd just killed a puppy. His eyes were wide when he saw me, but then he instantly dropped his gaze. "You okay?" he asked.

I nodded as I wrapped my arms around my chest. "I'll be fine. My dress...that's ruined." I winced. "Crap, I left it in your room." I moved to go back, but Bash's hand on my arm stopped me.

"I'll take care of it."

I slowly turned to look at him. "Thanks."

He shrugged before dropping his arm like touching me had burned him. "Let me walk you to your car," he said as he pulled open the front door.

I shook my head. "I'll be fine. Besides, I have your shirt now." I motioned toward his bare chest.

He glanced down and his cheeks flushed when he glanced back up at me. Then he frowned. "Are you sure?"

I nodded. "Yeah. I'll be fine. I've lived here a long time."

He studied me before stepping away from the door. "Okay."

I didn't bother to look at him as I walked past. I didn't allow myself to glance in my rearview mirror as I drove away. And I didn't allow myself to breathe until I was behind my front door and collapsing against the wall.

"Whoa, what happened to you?" Sabrina's voice caused me to jump and scream. Her eyes were wide as she stood there in a pair of adult onesie pajamas and an empty bottle in her hand.

I pinched my lips together and shook my head. She stared at me for a moment before murmured something about me being crazy under her breath and then disappeared into the kitchen.

I pressed my hand to my heart as I took in a deep breath. Whatever happened between Bash and me was over. I needed to stop myself from going down this path I was flirting with.

Bash was just a nice guy. That was all. And if I wasn't careful, I was going to ruin what I had with Anders. This was my first relationship in a long time and I was tired of ruining things.

I was ready to find my own happiness.

However that looked.

13

SHELBY

SWEET TEA &
SOUTHERN GENTLEMAN

I LEANED back against the headboard in my hotel room and took in a deep breath. I'd been here with Titan for the last twenty-four hours and I'd thought that being here in a beautiful Vermont resort would make me feel better...but it didn't.

Titan was the perfect doting, fake boyfriend. He picked me up from the airport with a huge bouquet of flowers and chocolates. His hug crushed me but his laugh made me smile. He was happy to see me, and things with him weren't complicated.

But I wasn't happy.

I was struggling to pretend. And now, I was headed to the rehearsal dinner, where I would act like we were in love and that I wasn't currently nursing a broken heart.

"Makeup," I murmured as I slipped off the bed and headed to my open suitcase. Maybe some more blush and darker eyeshadow would make it more believable that I'd walked away from the man I couldn't get out of my head.

I lifted my larger cosmetic bag from my suitcase and was headed over to the small vanity in the bathroom when a familiar floral pattern caught my attention. I glanced down to see that my grandmother's journal had been placed in my suitcase. Confused, I picked it up, and then realization dawned on me.

Abigail.

I sighed as I set the journal back down. But in the process, a piece of paper shifted from inside the front flap. I didn't remember there being any loose paper last time I shuffled through it, so I grasped the corner with my fingertips and pulled.

It was a note from Abigail.

Don't hate me for slipping this into your luggage, but I think there are some things in here that you need to know. If you're feeling up to it, flip through this. There's more to your past than you realize.

My entire mouth felt dry as I stared at Abigail's words. I felt betrayed that she'd read my grandmother's journal. I felt upset that she'd slipped this journal into my suitcase. And I hated that, even though I was mad at my friend, there was a part of me that wanted to know what the journal said.

I wanted to understand what had happened in my past.

Tears threatened to form, so I shook my head as I took

the journal and buried it deep in my suitcase. I didn't have the time to look through it. I needed to get ready to meet Titan in half an hour so we could emerge downstairs as the loving couple we were trying to be.

I needed to help him win back the woman he loved. If I wasn't going to have that for myself, I might as well help someone else find that happiness.

Somehow, I managed to ignore the weight of the journal the entire time I got ready. It wasn't until I was standing in front of the mirror, staring at my black dress and equally dark, smoky eye makeup that my curiosity won out.

I glanced over at the suitcase and gave in to the desire to flip it open and read what Abigail had read.

What she would risk our friendship over.

I sat down on the bed next to the suitcase and took a deep breath. I needed to be ready for whatever was written there. Whatever my grandmother thought was important enough that she wrote it down for me to find.

I needed to know what had happened when I walked away ten years ago.

I steeled my nerves as I slipped my hand underneath the clothes in my suitcase and found the hard cover of the journal. My fingers grasped it and I pulled it up and set it in my lap.

I ran my fingers over the swirls and petals of the flowers, laughing for a moment at how this designed screamed my grandmother. She loved flowers and doilies so much. But just as quickly as my smile had come, it disappeared. Pain clung to my chest as I remembered that night.

The night she stood on the porch of the inn while I shoved my luggage into my car, tears streaming down my face. It was dark and I couldn't see her reaction, but I assumed it was one of anger. She'd been disappointed in me. I'd followed in my mother's footsteps. I got pregnant. I'd convinced myself that my high school boyfriend was the man I was going to love forever.

She'd always wanted so much more for me, but I never lived up to her expectations.

She loved Miles more than she loved me because he never disappointed her like I had.

A tear dropped onto my fingers. I stared at it as it rolled off my skin and onto the journal. I wondered if my grandmother knew how much I cried for her. How much I cried for the past I'd walked away from. For the pain from losing my baby mixed with the pain of disappointing my grandmother. I'd wanted to be better, and yet I always felt like I'd failed her.

And she knew it. She watched it all from the porch of her beloved inn.

I blew out my breath as I grasped the edge of the journal and flipped it open to the title page. The familiarity of my grandmother's cursive washed over me. I ran my fingertips across the indentations made from her pen, tracing the words that were written.

To my dearest Shelby, may you find forgiveness for me in the pages of this journal.

A sob escaped my lips as I read the words. *Find forgiveness.* That seemed to be the theme of my life. I needed to find forgiveness for Miles. Gran needed to find forgiveness for me. I needed to find forgiveness for Gran. For my mom. For those in my life who hurt me.

Why was this so hard?

I tipped my face to the ceiling and closed my eyes. I'd held onto pain for so long that I wasn't sure how to let it go. Who was I if I wasn't Shelby, the girl who got pregnant in high school and then lost her baby. Who was I if I wasn't Shelby, granddaughter of Charlotte Cane, daughter of the woman who ran out of her family and then died in a car accident.

I was an accumulation of bad things, and I didn't know how to let all of that go and be a woman of good things.

Of love, openness...happiness.

I didn't know how to live in a world where I was content.

Three heavy knocks on my door startled me. I dropped the journal into my suitcase and stood.

"Shelby? You ready?" Titan's voice was muffled as he called through the door.

"Yeah, hang on," I replied as I hurried over to the mirror and grabbed a tissue. I didn't want to talk about the journal, my grandmother, or my past. This weekend was for Titan. I didn't want to bog him down with the stress I was feeling.

I took in a few deep breaths, blotted my smudged makeup, and forced a smile. When I pulled open the door, Titan's smile widened.

"You look amazing," he said.

My cheeks warmed. His gaze didn't have the same effect on me as Miles' did, but I was grateful that he was appreciative. "Thanks. We're going to knock Samantha's socks off."

Titan's expression turned serious. He swallowed, his Adam's apple bobbing up and down. "You think so?"

I nodded as I slipped my arm around his offered elbow. "Oh, man. She's going to be a goner." I bumped him with my shoulder. "I saw her staring at you earlier, in the lobby. She's still got it bad for you." We stood in front of the elevator, waiting for the doors to open. Titan tapped his foot on the ground. I chuckled. "Relax. We've got this."

My words must have left Titan's mind as soon as we got to the wedding venue. He'd seemed calm and collected when we climbed into his rental car and drove across town, but now, standing in the beautiful ceremony area lit up with twinkling lights, he was a nervous wreck.

I wanted to ask him why he didn't just tell Samantha how he felt, but I didn't think it was my place. I'd agreed to come, and I was a woman of my word. Even though I wasn't sure who I was or what my future held when I got back to Harmony Island, I was going to help Titan. It was the distraction I needed.

I linked arms with him as he led me over to the folding chairs that were set up for the ceremony, and we sat down. He adjusted his suit coat before blowing out his breath and looking at me for moral support. I patted his arm.

"You've got this."

His gaze drifted around the space, and I could tell the moment it landed on Samantha. His expression softened if only for a moment before he dropped it to study me. "This is the first time I'm going to have to be around her since we split up."

Memories of the first time I drove into Harmony Island after being gone for ten years flooded my mind. It was hard to face a past that meant so much to you.

"I get it. But remember, she's having to face it too." I offered him an encouraging smile.

He stared at me, and then his lips tipped up into a half smile. "You're right." And then his expression fell. "But what if our history meant more to me than it did to her? What if she's moved on?"

I stood and lifted my hands to his tie and adjusted it. Then I leaned in and pressed my lips to his cheek. "Then you hold your head high and know that I'm here to help you." I pulled back and smiled. "And you start the healing process."

He held my gaze before reaching out and giving me a

large, crushing hug. "Thanks for coming with me. I know it was strange, but I feel better with you here."

I patted his back. "That's what friends do."

He pulled back and stared down at me once more before he headed over to where the wedding planner was gathering the wedding party. I sat back in my chair and let out my breath. It was nice to focus on someone else's problems for once. Here, I wasn't the person with their heart on the line. What I said or did wouldn't affect my own happiness. If Titan ended up with his heart broken, I could help him save face.

At home, I was the vulnerable one. At home, it was my future and my past on the chopping block. At home, my heart was the one being broken.

———

TITAN DID BEAUTIFULLY. I panicked a bit for him when I saw the wedding planner pair him with Samantha, but he handled it with strength and grace, and I was fairly certain Samantha noticed. She kept staring at Titan as the wedding officiator walked the bride and groom through what was going to happen.

And there was a moment when he started walking back to me, that I saw her expression drop. She still had feelings for him. I could tell. And I couldn't wait to tell him.

When he saw me, he hugged me again, his body relaxing into mine. "That was torture," he murmured.

I laughed as I hugged him back, and then patted his shoulder when he pulled away. "I think it was more successful than you realize."

At my words, his gaze drifted over to Samantha. But then he brought it back and smiled down at me. "We're heading to the pub for drinks. Wanna go?"

Honestly, I wanted to go back to my room and wallow in self-pity while I stared at my grandmother's journal. But I figured that if I said those words, I would sound crazy, so I just smiled and nodded. "Sure."

The entire wedding party and their plus-ones took up half the space in the small pub. We were squished inside while the music blared and the bartenders shouted over it just to be heard. I found a small stool at the far end of the bar and claimed it for myself.

"I'll get us a drink," Titan shouted into my ear.

I nodded as he pushed through the crowd and over to where the bartender was taking orders. I slipped out my phone from my purse and glanced down at it. Disappointment clung to my chest when I saw that I had no message from Miles. I felt stupid for wanting him to message me. After all, I'd told him that we were over, why would he.

But there had been a part of me that thought he would be missing me. That he would reach out to see how I was.

I opened my text messages and hovered my thumb over his name before I shook my head and scrolled down to Abigail's number. I shot her a quick text, asking her how things were going and saying that I missed her, before I slipped my phone back into my purse. Titan appeared moments later with two bottles of beer.

"Here you are, m'lady," he said handing me a bottle.

I thanked him and took it. He stood next to me as we both took a drink. I glanced around, wondering where Samantha was and if he was wondering the same thing. It was hard to be here with him when I knew he wanted to be here with someone else.

"So, why aren't you—"

"I wonder where—"

We looked at each other. I gave him a sheepish smile. "You go ahead," I said.

He laughed and shrugged before he leaned in. "I was just wondering why you are here with me tonight and not out with some other guy."

I shook my head. "Well, my fake-dating calendar is quite booked up, but you were my first so..." I shrugged and took another drink.

He looked at me like he didn't believe me. "I should rephrase that. Why isn't there a boyfriend around to feel jealous that you agreed to fake-date me."

My eyes widened at his question.

"Not that I'm saying there couldn't be." He raised his hands like he was giving me a peace offering. "You're just beautiful and fun and interesting. I can't be the only guy who sees that."

My entire brain short-circuited at his words. Instantly, Miles' face entered my mind. Titan must have seen the change because he leaned closer. "There is a guy?"

I swallowed, my mouth turning dry from all of the emotions pulsating through me. I shook my head before taking a sip of beer.

"Who is this mystery man?" Titan asked, leaning closer to study me before pulling back and letting out a low whistle. "He's got his hooks in you bad."

I twisted my bottle of beer on the counter a few times as I stared at it. This wasn't how I was going to forget Miles. Talking about him like this was only going to do one thing...remind me that Miles meant something to me.

"Ah," Titan said as he nodded knowingly. "It's your person."

I blinked a few times. "My person?" I needed him to stop. Right now. Whatever he was going to say next would almost certainly break my heart. And my heart was so pulverized that talking about my feelings for Miles would grind the last little molecules into dust.

"Yeah, your person. They come into your life and change everything. You are no longer the person of your past, and you have no idea who future you is either. If your person is with you, you know you'll be safe. But if they aren't, you are so fundamentally changed that you're scared of moving forward without them." He leaned in once more, his gaze leveling with mine. "He's your life-altering person."

I knew I was staring at him, but I couldn't help it. It was as if someone finally verbalized exactly how I felt about Miles. How I'd been trying not to feel about him... but failing miserably.

I closed my eyes and shook my head. I didn't know how I was going to do any of the things I knew I needed to do. I needed to stay away from Miles, but also, I needed to be near him according to my grandmother's will. I needed to be cordial with him, but I didn't know how to be that person. Deep down, my feelings were so strong, I couldn't think of anything other than being with Miles.

"How do you move on?" I whispered, opening my eyes to see Titan watching me. He had a knowing look in his gaze like he knew exactly how I was feeling.

"You ask a stranger to be your date for a wedding so you can save face when she's there." His voice was soft, but his meaning wasn't lost on me. He scoffed as he tipped the beer against his lips and took a sip. "But that's just me."

My gaze drifted around the pub until it landed on Samantha. I caught her eye, and she dropped her gaze so fast, I almost wondered if I'd imagined it. But when she peered over at me, the look in her eyes confirmed what I already knew.

"I wouldn't say your plan was in vain," I said as I let out a fake laugh and punched his shoulder.

Titan looked down at where I'd struck him and then back up at me. "It wasn't?" His knitted brow told me he was confused, but thankfully, he knew enough to go along with it.

I leaned in until our cheeks were touching. "I think she's remembering what she had back when you two were together and regretting her choice to walk away." I pulled back and gave him a genuine smile.

He studied me before he slowly tipped his head to the side. I saw his gaze drift over in her direction before he brought it back to me. There was a glisten in his eye as he smiled. "Well, if there's hope for me, then there's hope for you."

His response caused my smile to falter. If Titan noticed, he didn't say so. Instead, he downed the rest of his drink and then started to dance a few inches away from me. He was riding high, but I was left digesting his words.

Truth was, I wanted there to be hope for me and Miles. But from where I was sitting, there was no chance. Not when there was a chance for him and Tamara to get together and for Belle to have an intact family.

So, sure, Titan may have a chance with Samantha. I truly hoped things worked out for them. But for me and my love life—my person. That just wasn't in the cards.

Now or ever.

14

SHELBY

SWEET TEA &
SOUTHERN GENTLEMAN

I WOKE up the next morning aching and hungover. After our serious conversation last night at the pub, we ordered another round of beers, and that seemed to do the trick. We both let our hair down and danced like no one was watching. I stumbled into my hotel room at two in the morning and passed out on the bed.

"Never again," I whispered before I winced at the taste of beer and sleep on my tongue. I needed to brush my teeth something awful.

I managed to make my way over to the bathroom and into the shower. Once I was clean and had fresh breath, I felt better. I wrapped myself up in a huge, fluffy towel and then used my hand to wipe away the condensation on the mirror.

I used a makeup towelette to clean off the mascara on my cheeks and then smeared a face mask all over my skin.

While that sat, I padded out to my bed, made it quick, and then settled down for a little morning meditation.

I closed my eyes as I sat there, the memory of my conversation with Titan floating around in my mind. He was right, even though it hurt to admit. Miles was my person. It felt like the universe was trying to say something to me, but I was struggling to understand what that was.

We'd grown up together. We'd protected each other. At every point in our life, we seemed to manage to make it back to each other. Was I fighting against something that was so meant to be that it was written in our future?

I closed my eyes and took in a deep cleansing breath. I struggled with the idea of Miles' and my happiness coming before Belle's. It felt like a betrayal of myself. I would have loved it if my mom and dad could have made it work. Hell, I would have loved it if my mom and Miles' dad could have made it work. But it seemed like I was destined to be fatherless forever.

I didn't want that for Belle.

I didn't want that for myself.

I shook my head as I opened my eyes. I was getting tired of trying to convince my heart that I couldn't be with Miles. It was exhausting to find the strength to move on, only for my head and heart to betray me and yank me back into this cyclone of uncertainty.

Was I ever going to be able to move on?

Titan's words flooded my mind as I sat there. I was scared of my future and what that looked like without

Miles in it. Without my life in New York in it. I needed to figure out who Shelby was. And to find out who Shelby was, I needed to face my past. Move on from the chains of my past decisions.

I slitted my eyes and peeked over at my suitcase, knowing what I needed to do. I couldn't speak to my grandmother, but I could read her words to me. And maybe, just maybe, if I read them, I would find it in myself to move on from the hurt and betrayal that filled my soul.

I slipped off the bed and made my way to my suitcase. After dressing in a pair of yoga pants and an oversized t-shirt, I grabbed her journal and made my way back to the bed, where I propped myself up with pillows and covered myself with a throw blanket I'd found in the closet.

I flipped open to the title page and allowed my fingers to run across her handwriting once more.

To my dearest Shelby, may you find forgiveness for me in the pages of this journal.

I sucked in my breath as I realized that I was about to embark on an emotional journey that was going to fundamentally change who I was and the future ahead of me. I played with the corner of the paper, wavering between the desire to rip this bandage off and the desire to stay in the dark. Finally, I shook my head and turned the page.

My dearest Shelby,

Last night you drove away. I must say, I'm still in shock. I wanted to go after you, but I fear that will only push you farther away from me. I can only pray that, some-

day, you'll forgive me for the pain I've caused you, and someday we'll sit on the porch of the inn like we did before, drinking tea and laughing.

For now, I'll sit here with my broken heart, praying that you will be safe and find happiness wherever you land.

Love you lots,

Gran

Tear brimmed my eyes as I stared down at her words and the familiarity of her loopy cursive. I ran my fingers over her words as I read them over and over again. I'd always thought she didn't love me. That she was grateful to get rid of me. That I was nothing but a reminder of the daughter who broke her heart and saddled her with two children she didn't ask for.

But sitting here, reading these words, made me think differently.

I turned the page and kept reading.

Dear Shelby,

It's been a week since you left, and I ran into that loud-mouth Missy at Godwin's. She looked so smug that it took all the Christian woman I had in me not to smack her face right there in the cereal aisle. She should have never treated you like that. It was her son's fault for treating you that way. Miles told me what Clint did to you, and when he finished, my blood was boiling.

I'm so grateful you and Miles had each other. He really cares about you and is determined to protect you. I know you felt betrayed by him, but he really did what he thought was right. I hope someday the two of you will find each other again. That you will always protect each other.

My eyes were so full of tears that I couldn't see. I closed my eyes and tipped my head back as a sob escaped my lips. I had failed so epically in my life, and I was grieving.

I was grieving the baby I lost that night. I was grieving the loss of my grandmother. I was grieving the time I spent running away from my past, thinking that no one wanted me around, when in fact the two people who were my family wanted me back.

They'd missed me as much as I'd missed them.

I lost myself in my grandmother's words. Her journal entries turned from ones of sadness and regret to ones of hope and the town's gossip. It was like reading the history of the town over the last decade. Who was getting married. Who was having babies...who was cheating. I could hear my grandmother's voice as I read her words, and with each journal entry, the pain that I carried around for her and the past lessened.

Until suddenly, all I wanted was to go back to Harmony. To be closer to the people who raised me. To live the life that I grieved. Now was the time to start living. Now was the time to push myself out of the cave of grief and pain and stand in the sunrise of my new life.

I was tired of living for the past.

I wanted my future to look different.

My phone chimed with a text message. I startled and

glanced down to see that it was from Titan. He was asking me if I was almost ready for the wedding. Realizing that I'd been reading for over an hour, I shot back a thumbs-up and then scrambled off the bed and into the bathroom to do my makeup and hair.

There was a knock on my door as I shimmied into my dress and pulled it up over my shoulders. I could only get the zipper up halfway, so I hurried over to the door and pulled it open.

Titan was a sight to behold. If he wasn't so incredibly hung up on Samantha, and I wasn't...whatever I was with Miles, there would be a definite attraction there. My eyes were wide as my gaze met his. He looked equally startled as his jaw dropped open.

"Jeez, Shelby. You clean up good."

I swatted his arm before grabbing his hand and pulling him into my hotel room. I pulled my curled hair away from my neck and waved toward my zipper. "Can you help me?"

He chuckled as he stepped closer to me and grasped my zipper. The warmth of his fingers sent shivers down my back. Suddenly, I was standing in Miles' bathroom, waiting for him to help me get out of my dress.

My heart surged at the memory. I wanted Miles. All of him. I wanted him to be here with me. I wanted him to help me with my dress. I wanted to be there to help him with the inn. To help him with Belle.

I wanted to be his person like he was for me.

My entire body stiffened as I stood there, not knowing what I was going to say. I couldn't go to this wedding with Titan. Not when all I wanted to do was board a plane or rent a car and drive all night to see Miles.

"There you go," Titan said as he finished pulling up my zipper.

I hoped he would understand what I needed to do as I slowly turned to face him. He was smiling at me, but as soon as he took in my expression, his face fell.

"You need to go," he said, his voice low.

I chewed on my bottom lip. "I have to." I stepped forward and flung my arms around his neck. "But you've got this. If I didn't think you did, I would stay." I pulled back so that I could study him. "Listen to me, don't wait ten years in grief just to come to the conclusion that you should have never let Samantha walk away. Stop her now. Tell her now that you love her. Start your future now."

With each word, the weight I'd carried for so long got lighter and lighter. "She's your person. You are fundamentally changed because of her. Tell her that. Don't let her continue thinking that you don't care, because you do. Being brave in love...it's the only pure thing we can do as humans." I brought my hand up to his cheek and held it there. "It's the only thing that makes us truly alive."

He held my gaze and then nodded. "I'll be brave and tell her." He held up his finger. "Only if you promise me that you'll do the same."

I sucked in my breath as I took a step back. I waggled my finger in his direction. "Ooo, that's dirty."

He shrugged before he shoved his hands into the front pockets of his tux. "It's only fair. If I do it, so should you."

I glared at him. "You don't understand. There are more people involved than just me and him."

Titan studied me for a moment before he nodded. "I get it." He clicked his tongue as he looked around. "How about this," he said, bringing his gaze back to me. "How about, if fate puts you in a situation where you can say the words, you have to tell him."

I mulled over that challenge. I was starting to believe a little deeper in fate. In things happening for a reason. So I was willing to accept his terms. I held out my hand. "I promise." He grasped my hand and shook it. I didn't let go right away. Instead, I pulled his hand closer. "But you have to promise me that you'll tell Samantha."

He nodded.

"Tonight."

He narrowed his eyes. "Tonight?"

"Tonight," I repeated.

He studied me before he nodded. "Fine. I'll do it tonight."

I rose up on my tiptoes and placed a kiss on his cheek. I gave him a small smile when I lowered back down onto my heels. "Thanks," I said.

He frowned. "For what?"

"For helping me figure out my crap. For giving me a

place to land when I needed it and listening to me while I drunk-vented."

He laughed. "Of course. And thanks for being my plus-one when I needed it."

"Anytime."

He was stepping around me, but stopped when I spoke. He glanced down at me and shook his head. "Hopefully, this is the last time."

I turned and followed him to the door, holding it open as he passed through. "It will be the last time. Samantha is in love with you. Go get her."

He chuckled as he gave me a small salute. "Yes, ma'am." Then his expression turned serious. "Have a safe trip back to Harmony."

I blew out my breath as I realized what I was going to have to do to get back. "Will do."

I watched him walk down the hall. And when he turned the corner and disappeared, my shoulders slumped. I was ready to get out of this dress and into my sweats. I had a flight to catch, and if that didn't work, I had a long drive home.

Home.

I stopped just as I closed my hotel door. That word. That one four-letter word. *Home.* I smiled as I moved to grab my phone.

I was going home.

15

ABIGAIL

I WAS FLOUNDERING WITHOUT SHELBY. I really hadn't thought it would be this hard with her gone. After all, I'd pretty much run the shop by myself for years. But there was something going on in the town, and my shop was packed to the brim in the morning, and I was desperately trying to stock my shelves for the afternoon and evening rush.

I was sweating like a pig when the last group of construction workers left the shop and I was able to take a deep breath.

The nice thing about being so busy was that I didn't have time to think about Anders or Bash—especially Bash. Everything that had transpired between us last night left me feeling extremely confused. I wanted to play his actions off as him being a kind roommate, but deep down, I couldn't.

I saw the way he looked at me. I saw the heat in his gaze. I felt how close he stood to me.

There was something there, even if I doubted Bash would ever do anything about it. He was loyal to Anders, and as far as he knew, Anders wanted me and I wanted Anders.

Which had been true, until...

The front door bell jingled, startling me. For a split second, I hoped that it was Anders and Bash walking through the door so I could figure out exactly how I felt about what was happening. But I was met with the frazzled expression that only Missy could pull off.

Grateful that Shelby was far away in Vermont, I forced a smile and approached the register. From the fire in Missy's gaze, I knew I was in for a story.

"How's your morning going?" I asked as I punched in her order of regular coffee with two sugars.

Missy blew out her breath as she leaned against the counter. "I'm so worn out. I've been all over town, plus the bed and breakfast is just bursting at the seams." She tucked her normally perfectly coiffed hair back up into a bun. She leaned over the counter and studied me. "I'm telling you this because you're a business owner, and it's important that you know. I just got back from the mayor's office."

She waggled her finger in front of my face. "I was over there telling him how crazy it is that there are so many construction workers here. I mean, there's supporting the local economy, and then there's running us ragged." She drummed her fingers on the countertop. "I ain't young no more. I can't keep working like this."

I nodded as I snapped the lid onto her filled coffee cup and then slid it across to her. "I hear you. I can barely keep things in stock."

Missy grasped the coffee cup with both hands as she glanced around. "They're even buying books?"

I glanced in the direction she was looking. My bookshelves were looking a little barren. Which made my heart surge. I loved that people were buying books. "It's amazing."

Missy snapped her gaze back to me. "Well, when you hear what I'm about to tell you, you won't think it's so amazing."

I gave her my focus as I waited for her to spill the latest gossip.

"The mayor just informed me that some billion-dollar investment company is planning to buy out downtown Harmony. They're looking to turn this into some southern Martha's Vineyard place. An exclusive destination." She leaned closer. "They're fixing to kick us all out."

I raised my eyebrows. I could normally trust Missy's gossip. She was meticulous before she spread anything. She told me her word was gold, and she wouldn't taint it with untrue things.

So her saying these things confused me. I hadn't heard

of anyone wanting to buy The Shop Around the Corner. Since I was in downtown Harmony, I would expect to be in the first wave of offers. Then again, the vast number of construction workers did give credibility to her words. But still, it seemed too Hollywood for an investment company to come in and buy up the entire town.

"That's incredible," I said as I opened the display case and removed a chocolate chip cookie. "I haven't had anyone offer to buy the shop, so I guess maybe they haven't started handing out the offers?"

Missy nodded as she took the cookie from me. "Nothing has been finalized, but Harold said that it's in the works for them to purchase the town outright. Then, we'll be seeing the offers to purchase the property." Missy leaned in. "From what I'm hearing, they are going to demolish everything and start from scratch." She clutched the front of her shirt. "Not the Apple Blossom, though. They are going to have to pry it from my cold, dead fingers first."

I nodded along with her words. I loved this little shop. I loved this town. I had friends here. I had a place to belong. I wasn't in any hurry to sell it off. "Yeah, I'm not interested in selling."

Missy stared at me, causing me to pull back slightly. "Do you swear you won't sell?"

I blinked, not sure how to take her intensity. "Um, yeah."

She narrowed her eyes as if she were trying to catch me in a lie. She studied me for a moment longer before she pulled back. "Good. I'm glad to have you in my corner." She gathered her coffee and half-eaten cookie. "Now, if you'll excuse me, I have more people to talk to."

I watched her walk across the shop. Just as she pushed open the door, the bell jingling once more, she paused and peered over her shoulder at me. "If we all agree we won't sell, there's nothing they can do."

I gave her a small salute, and that seemed to appease her. She walked out onto the sidewalk and disappeared around the corner. I leaned against the counter with my arms crossed, chewing on her words. I had a feeling things in this town were about to be shook up. What that meant for Harmony and the small shops that thrived on the local economy was a mystery. And honestly, it was a shake-up that I wasn't looking forward to.

My life felt like it was on a fault line already.

I was so grateful when Fanny walked in at six. I was exhausted and ready to take a shower and curl up on my bed with a romantic comedy and a box of cereal. Life was really taking a toll on me, and I just hoped that Sabrina was having another good day so I wouldn't have to watch Samuel for her.

I was ready for some me time.

I was in my office, trying to finish my food order when Fanny found me and pointed her finger in my direction and then to the door. I tried to protest, but she wasn't having any of it. Instead, she stayed by me like my shadow until I headed out to my car and turned the engine on.

I felt like a zombie as I drove home. When I pulled into the parking lot, I glanced up at our windows to see that everything was dark.

"That's strange," I mumbled as I grabbed my purse and climbed out of the car. Maybe Sabrina and Samuel were asleep.

That wasn't normal, but nothing about our life had been normal for a very long time. I was starting to get used to the curveballs.

I yawned as I walked up the stairs to our front door and shoved the key into the lock. All I could think about was drinking some hot chocolate as I soaked in the tub. I pushed open the door and stepped inside, kicking my shoes off as I went.

"I'm home," I called out to the darkness that surrounded me. I frowned as I turned around and shut the door behind me. Then I flipped on the living room light. "Sabrina?"

Nothing.

I glanced around, hoping to maybe see Samuel in his bassinet.

Nothing.

My heart began to pound, but I shushed it as I walked through the apartment, checking first Sabrina's room and then my own. Finally, when Samuel's room came up empty, my ability to keep my panic in check faltered, and I ran through each room one more time just to make sure I hadn't missed anything.

When I came back to the kitchen, I knew that something was very wrong.

Sabrina was gone.

I dug through my purse, my hands shaking as I searched for my phone. Once I had it grasped in my hands, I swiped it on. Seconds later, her number was dialing.

Ring.

Ring.

I looked up.

Ring.

Ring.

I swore under my breath. I could hear her phone ringing from her bedroom, which I knew was empty. I'd overturned everything when I was in there the second time.

Realizing that was a dead end, I hung up the phone and punched in 9-1-1. It only took a few seconds for the dispatcher to pick up.

"He–llo," I said, my voice coming out panicked and breathy. "I need to report a missing person."

"Yes, ma'am. How long have they been missing?"

I shook my head, tears filling my eyes. "I don't know. My sister was here this morning and now she's gone."

There was a pause.

"So you're saying that she was with you this morning and now is gone?"

"With my nephew."

"Uh huh." Deep sigh. "Did the two of you fight? Is there a chance that the father to her son wanted to spend some time with them? I mean, sisters do argue and need space from each other."

I pulled back, blinking hard as I tried to make sense of what she said. "My sister and I live together with her son. We have a good relationship. We weren't fighting. I mean she was struggling for a while now, but she has no place to go. Her phone's here and..." I glanced around to see her purse hanging next to the door. "And her purse is here."

"Right, ma'am. I understand that you're worried. But people have the right to leave their residence without their phone or purse. Sometimes, it's just best to wait a bit longer to see if they turn up." She clicked her tongue. "They always do."

I wanted to fight. I wanted to scream. This wasn't like Sabrina. She was struggling and she needed help. My blood boiled as I hung up on the dispatcher just as I heard her whisper under her breath, "If I get another *True Crime* watcher call me, Imma quit."

Feeling alone, I wanted to call Shelby, but she wasn't here and I didn't want to stress her out. There was nothing she could do.

I pulled my shoes back on and hurried out the door.

The only thing I could think of was to head over to Anders' to see if he'd help me put together a search party. I had to look for her.

Darkness had crept up around me as I pulled onto his street. There was only a lone light on in his apartment and I prayed that he was home. I threw the car into park, grabbed my purse, hurried up the stairs, and banged on their front door.

"Anders!" I yelled as I continued to knock. I became more frantic the longer it was taking him to answer. He had to be home. I needed help. I couldn't search all of Harmony and the surrounding towns for Sabrina on my own.

Where would she have gone? And with Samuel? A sob escaped my lips. I was just praying that my nephew was safe. If anything happened to him, I would never forgive myself.

The door moved from under my hand and I stumbled forward.

Bash's eyes were wide as he stared down at me. He was shirtless and wore a pair of pajama pants. His hair was tousled like he'd been sleeping. "What the hell?" he asked as he folded his arms and stared down at me.

I didn't give him an explanation even though I could feel his irritation. "Is Anders here?" I asked as I pushed past him and into the apartment.

"Abigail, what's wrong?" His hand was on my elbow, stopping me in my tracks.

Another sob escaped my lips. "Is Anders here?" I asked again. I was exhausted and worried, and I was in the wrong headspace to try to analyze what was going on between us.

I needed some normalcy and, right now, that was Anders.

Bash pulled his hand back as he shook his head. "No. I think he went to the pub."

I glanced up at him. His eyebrows were furrowed as he stared down at me. I chewed my lip as I nodded. "I'll go find him there, then." I moved to step past him, and I could feel it as his body turned with me.

"Anything I can help with?" he asked as I grasped the door handle.

I shook my head. "My sister and my nephew are missing. I need help finding them." I glanced over my shoulder at him. "You were sleeping. It's okay. Anders and I will find him."

Bash's gaze darkened. "You don't think I can help?"

I let out my breath as I closed my eyes for a moment. "It's fine. It's a job for my boyfriend." The word tasted bitter on my tongue, but I needed whatever this was between Bash and me to stop. After all, he was dark and brooding and confusing.

I needed someone consistent and uncomplicated in my life. I think I'd gotten swept away in the romanticism of Bash. The dark, mysterious guy who, in the end, just breaks your heart.

I was tired of feeling alone, and I wasn't sure Bash was the kind of guy who stuck around.

"Right," he said as he reached over my head to hold the door open. "Your boyfriend is down at the pub. It shouldn't be too hard for you to find him."

I nodded—a bit too frantically—and headed out into the hall. I turned to thank him, but I was met with a shutting door. Startled, I stood there, staring at the wood before I snapped out of my stupor and headed down the hall.

I didn't like the sick feeling I had in my stomach, but the words needed to be said. My life was complicated enough with Sabrina and the shop, I didn't need to add another person into my circle who was just going to confuse me all the time.

Sure, Anders completely ignored me the other night, but his intentions with me were straightforward—and I needed that.

I drove all the way to the pub, and my heart was racing as I pulled into the parking lot and climbed out of my car. Just as I started walking toward the pub, my phone rang. I glanced down, hoping it was the police, but Dad's face flashed on my screen.

I'd try to call him on my way over to the pub, but he didn't answer. My entire body heated as I swiped the phone on and brought it to my cheek.

"Dad?"

Silence. "Abi?"

"Dad," I said again as the dam broke inside of me causing the tears to flow.

"What's wrong?"

"It's Sabrina. She's taken Samuel and I can't find her." My words were broken up with sobs, and I feared that he couldn't hear me.

"We're getting in the car and coming. Hang tight."

I nodded, but he couldn't see me. He hung up the phone, and I let mine fall from my shoulder as I stuffed it back into my purse.

Dad was coming. It would be some time, but he would be here to help. That's what I needed to focus on.

The music inside was blaring as I approached the front doors. The cool metal of the door handle stung my skin, and just when I went to pull, the door whipped open, throwing me off balance.

"Sorry." The man who was barreling through tossed the apology in my direction, but I didn't respond.

I needed to find Anders and get searching.

Thankfully, Jax was working the bar. He owned Harmony Pub, and he kept close tabs on who was coming in and going out of the place. If Anders was here, he'd know it.

I pushed my way through the crowd and up to the counter. I leaned over it, waving my hand in the hopes that I would catch Jax's attention before he was swept away with some drunk girl's order.

It worked. He saw me, nodded, and headed in my

direction. "Hey, Abigail. I've been reading that book I bought last week." He winked at me. "I think I've figured out who the killer is...what's wrong?" My expression must have finally registered because his smile faded as he began to look around. "Are you in trouble?"

I nodded but then shook my head. "My sister..."

"Sabrina?"

"Yeah, she's missing."

Jax looked toward the door. "I haven't seen her come in here."

I waved away his comment. "I doubt she's here. I'm looking for Anders. He's like this tall"—I stepped away from the counter and rose up onto my tiptoes—"he has blond hair. Is a construction worker."

Jax blew out his breath. "With all the commotion around town, that describes just about every new guy in here." He glanced over the crowd and then waved toward the back, where the pool tables where. "I'd check over there. That's where the majority of them seem to congregate."

I nodded and turned, but he leaned forward and grabbed my arm. "How can I help?"

I stopped and peered back at him. "If she comes in here, call me."

He straightened as he gave a salute. "Yes, ma'am. I close the bar at two. If you're still searching, call me. I'll come help find her."

Tears flooded my eyes once more. I prayed that I

wouldn't still be searching at two a.m. but it was a possibility. One that I wasn't sure I was ready to face.

"Hopefully, we'll be back home, tucked into bed, and this will all be a bad memory."

He nodded. "I agree."

Not wanting to waste any more time, I gave him a quick smile and pushed through the crowd until I found the pool tables. Jax had been right. I found Anders, drunk and about ready to fight another pool player with his pool cue. Luckily, I grabbed it away from him before he was able to use it as a weapon.

Anders startled and glared down at me. I grabbed his arm and pulled him away from the table so we could talk.

"I need your help," I shouted over the music.

Anders stared at me. "Abigail?"

I nodded. "Sabrina is missing. I need your help to find her."

"Sss-abrina?" He slurred the *s* and covered me in a cloud of alcohol.

I pulled back, frustration filling my chest. This entire trip had been futile. He was too drunk to help me. There was no way he was going to be able to drive. And if he came with me, I'd spend the night helping him puke on the side of the road.

I pushed him back toward the table. "You're drunk," I said, failing to mask the hurt that I felt. I began to stalk away, but his hands found my hips and then I was being pulled into him.

"Come on, baby. Don't leave. We can have fun here." His words were hot on my neck.

Heat pricked at my skin from anger and the proximity of his body to mine. I didn't want any of this. It wasn't sexy or attractive. He was supposed to support me. How could he do that when he couldn't even walk in a straight line.

"Get off me," I said as I shoved his hands away.

That threw him off balance for a split second before he was coming right back. "Come on, baby."

I shook my head and tried to wiggle away, but his hands remained. Suddenly, he was being shoved to the side. I let out a yelp as I sprang free of Anders' hands.

"I think you're done here," Jax's voice was deep and menacing. I must have looked shocked, because Jax crouched down to meet my gaze. "You okay?"

I nodded.

"Go find your sister. I'll take care of your boyfriend. He can sleep his hangover off in my office."

"Thanks," I whispered.

Jax nodded then grabbed Anders by the arm and began pushing him back toward the bar. I didn't wait to see where he brought him. I pulled my purse strap higher up on my shoulder and hurried out of the pub.

Once I was in my car and driving down the street, I let out a sob. That was not how I'd wanted that to go. I wanted—no, needed—someone here with me. I felt so alone. So small in this giant world.

I feared what I was going to find once I located

Sabrina. I hoped that she and Samuel were safe, but I'd seen enough true crime documentaries to know that was the exception, not the rule.

I just hoped that I could find her before she did anything she might regret.

16

ABIGAIL

SWEET TEA &
SOUTHERN GENTLEMAN

AN HOUR HAD PASSED and I still hadn't found Sabrina. I combed the streets of Harmony and even ventured out to the surrounding towns looking for her.

With each passing minute, my heart grew heavier and heavier.

Where could she have gone? She didn't know anyone. It's not like she spent a lot of time outside of the house even.

And with Samuel? Why would she take him and leave?

A sob escaped my lips as I continued to drive. I couldn't stop to cry. I couldn't stop to feel sorry about myself. I needed to keep going even though my entire body wanted to quit on me.

"Where are you?" I called out to the ether. I slammed my hands on the steering wheel and screamed.

I should have never left her. I should have tried harder. I should have gotten her help. I was her sister. I should have been better.

Just as I gripped the wheel, a loud popping noise filled the air, and suddenly, the car began to slow. I stared ahead as smoke billowed from the hood of my car. Not wanting to end up in the middle of the road, I pulled onto the shoulder and just sat there.

I was in shock. Shock that my sister was missing. But fate was a beast and landed me yet another blow.

"Are you serious?" I whispered. I wanted to scream and hit someone, but I didn't know who. I was literally alone in the middle of the highway in the dark. And I hadn't found my sister.

My hands shook as I found the hood release and then pulled open the door and stepped out. I had no idea what I was going to do, but I had to try something. I coughed as I rounded the car and pulled the hood up. Smoke billowed around me, but thankfully, it only lasted for a few seconds before it cleared and I was able to stare down at the engine.

I couldn't tell what the problem was. I was no mechanic. I knew how to put in windshield washer fluid and that was about it. Beyond that, I was at a complete loss.

I grabbed my phone out of my back pocket and swiped it on. Who could I call? Anders was sleeping off his beer in Jax's office. Shelby was in Vermont. There was no way Dad could make it to me anytime soon...so I was alone.

I opened my contact information, and a few names down I stopped. Bash's name sat there like a bright, blinking red light. Anders had put his phone number in my contacts the first night we hung out after he got back. He wanted me to have access to him in case something happened. My finger hovered over his name for a moment before I mustered my courage and pressed on it.

He might not like it, but he was the only person in the town who I knew well enough to call and ask for help. And if he didn't answer or refused to come, I'd find someone else to help me, even if that meant hitchhiking.

"Hello?"

My heart stopped as Bash's deep voice filled my head. "Bash?"

Pause.

"Abigail?"

"I need your help. I'm..." I took a deep breath. "I'm on highway 80. My car's smoking, and I don't know what's wrong. I haven't been able to find Sabrina and I'm freaking out. I went to the pub to find Anders, and he was drunk, and now..." Suddenly, I felt drops of rain hitting my head. "Now it's raining on me." The words came out a whisper as I closed my eyes.

This evening couldn't get any worse.

The sound of a feminine voice in the background made me stand up straight. I stared hard at the ground.

Was he with someone? Is that why he pushed me from the apartment so fast?

"Oh my gosh," I said as I wrapped my arm around my stomach. I wanted to puke and scream at the same time. "You're with someone. I'll just—" I didn't even finish. Instead, I just pulled my phone from my cheek and clicked the end call button.

I tried to shield my hair from the rain as I hurried to the driver's door and pulled it open. I collapsed on the seat and leaned forward with both hands on the wheel and just cried. I felt so stupid and defeated and weak.

My car was broken, and I had no clue if I was even going to be able to fix it. Sabrina was missing and now it was raining. And deep down—in a stupid part of my brain —I was a little heartbroken that Bash was with another woman.

Everything was very, very wrong right now.

My phone vibrated. I glanced down to see that it was Bash calling me back. I shook my head as I let it go to voicemail. Once he was finished saying whatever he was going to say, I texted him.

Me: Hey, don't worry, you sound like you're busy. I'll just contact a tow truck driver.

I set my phone down, trying to convince myself that I didn't really care if he answered or not. Instead, I just closed my eyes and took in some deep, cleansing breaths. But as soon as my phone lit up, I was picking it up.

Bash: Where on 80 are you?

Me: I think I remember exit 195, but really, it's no big deal. You don't have to come. I'll find someone else.

A few seconds later, he responded.

Bash: Okay

I stared at that one little word. *Okay?* What did that mean? Okay, he's coming? Or, okay, call a tow truck.

I cursed his name as I tossed my phone onto the passenger seat and folded my arms. I was going to feel sorry for myself for exactly one minute, and then I was going to do something about my situation.

Time ticked by, and my anxiety to find Sabrina overtook my frustration with Bash. When my minute was up, I'd successfully pushed my thoughts about him to the back of my mind and I was now focused on the reason I was out here on this road—to find my sister.

I opened my web browser on my phone and started searching for tow trucks in the area. I wasn't sure exactly where I was, but there had to be one somewhere. I located one and pressed the phone number listed. It rang, but all I got was an answering machine, so I left a message with my name and number.

Each number I called went to voicemail. So I left the same information. Once I'd run out of people to call, I set my phone down and closed my eyes. Stress permeated my body, but there really wasn't anything I could do. I had to sit tight and pray that Sabrina would randomly call me and everything would be fine.

It was a long shot, but it was the only hope I had.

I wasn't sure how much time had passed, but when my phone rang, I startled. I grabbed for my phone and swiped to answer the call without even looking at the caller ID.

"Yes, hello?" I asked, desperate for it to be a tow truck company and not some spammer.

"Mrs. Orion?"

I paused. I didn't remember leaving my last name in the messages, but maybe I did. "This is she."

"This is Claudette Longly at Harmony Medical Center..."

My entire body went numb. "Yeah?"

"I'm calling you because your sister, Sabrina, gave us your number as a contact for her. Is that right?"

"Sabrina? Is she there?"

"Yes, sweetheart. She was dropped off about fifteen minutes ago."

My stomach churned. "And Samuel?"

As if he'd heard the sound of his name, a wail sounded in the background. "He's here and vocal."

My entire body collapsed against the seat as relief filled my body. They were found. They were safe. They were alive.

"Thank you for calling me. Thank you...thank you..." I whispered as I lost all strength to speak.

"Well, head on over here. We're running some tests and getting vitals on both, but they are here and they are waiting for you."

I nodded, tears filling my eyes to the point that my

entire vision was blurred. She hung up, but I just sat there with my phone pressed to my cheek as I stared out at the rain hitting the windshield in front of me.

Sabrina was alive. She was safe. Samuel was just fine from the way he was wailing in the background. This entire nightmare was over. Sabrina was home and I wasn't going to stop until she got the help that she needed.

I dialed dad's number, and we both cried in relief that she was found. He said that he and Penny were still coming down to make sure that the two of us were safe. I told him I loved him and to drive safe. A pair of headlights came up from behind me just as I hung up the phone.

I glanced in my rearview mirror as the lights grew closer and closer until they stopped right behind me. I glanced over my shoulder, wondering if it was an axe murderer coming to take me out, or if one of the towing companies was telepathic and knew right where to find me.

The driver's door opened, so I moved to open mine as well. I stepped out and saw a dark figure walking toward me. As soon as they stepped out of the haze of the headlights, I saw that it was Bash. My instincts set in and I ran up to him and threw my arms around him.

He froze as I hugged him, but I didn't care. I'd gone from panic to relief in the last few minutes, and I just needed to hold someone and to have them hold me back. As if the shock had worn off, he leaned into me, wrapping his arms around my waist and pulling me to his chest.

"She's safe," I whispered into his chest.

I felt his cheek press against my head as he tightened his hold on me. "Sabrina?" he whispered, sending shivers down my back.

I nodded. "And Samuel is safe." I closed my eyes and breathed in the scent that I'd surrounded myself with last night when he loaned me his clothes.

"That's good news, right?" he asked.

I loved the rumbling I felt from his chest as he spoke. His grip was tight and possessive. Like he wasn't going to let me go.

"It's great news," I said as I pulled back to look at him.

He lifted his head to study me. Suddenly, his fingertips grazed my cheek as he wiped a tear away. "Why are you crying then?" His gaze met mine and I wanted to melt. He was worried about me. He...cared about me.

"I felt so alone and worried. But now...now she's safe." I didn't pull my gaze away. I wanted to swim in the dark, blue of his eyes.

"I'm sorry you felt alone," he said.

"I'm not anymore. You're here."

He furrowed his brow, and his gaze searched mine. Before he responded, he pulled back, pushing his hand through his hair and dropping his gaze. "You called me. What else was I supposed to do." He sucked in his breath as he glanced around. "Besides, Anders would have my head if he knew I left his girl on the side of the road in the rain." He waved toward his truck. "Let me give you a lift."

I felt so cold after he pushed me away, but the chilliness helped smack some sense into me. What was I doing holding my boyfriend's best friend like that? I was going to blame that reaction on my exhaustion and leave it at that.

Bash didn't look like he wanted to talk about it, and truthfully, neither did I. I'd felt alone and vulnerable. Of course I was going to hug the first person who came my way...

Right?

"Let me grab my purse out of the car and I'll meet you at your truck," I called over my shoulder as I hurried to the driver's door and opened it. I gathered my stuff from the front seat and then slammed the door behind me.

Bash was already behind the wheel by the time I climbed into his truck. He had the heat blasting, which I appreciated. As soon as I was settled, he handed me a blanket. He must have caught my confused stare, because he glanced over at me for a moment before he turned on his blinker and pulled into the nearest lane.

"I used to live in my truck," he said nonchalantly. Like that explanation was normal.

"I'm sorry, what?" I asked as I tucked the blanket under my legs and behind my body.

He sighed as he rested his wrist on the steering wheel and settled back into his seat. I continued to stare at him, expecting a response. He glanced back at me a few times before he shifted in his seat again and sighed.

"Let's just say that there's a lot about me that you don't know." He shrugged as he changed lanes. "And I'm not one to talk about it."

I studied him a bit longer, hoping that my stare would pressure him to talk, but it failed. Instead, he kept his gaze on the road as we drove into Harmony. By the time he pulled into the medical center's parking lot, he seemed antsy for me to go.

I thought about asking him if he wanted to come in, but then I felt stupid. He probably left his girlfriend at the apartment to come pick me up and was ready to get back to her.

"Thanks for coming to get me," I said as I grasped my purse to my body and opened the door. "Tell your girl that I appreciate her sharing you with me." I jumped to the ground.

Bash was staring at me with a confused expression. "Who?"

I waved away his question. "Whoever was talking in the background when I called you. I'm sure you're ready to get back to her." I gave him a soft smile, hoping he knew that I appreciated what he'd done for me. I had no intention of taking any more of his time.

He frowned, but then a look of understanding passed over his face. "Oh."

"Thanks, Bash," I said as I stepped back and slammed the door. I didn't want him to feel like he needed to give me more information. And if I were honest with myself, I didn't really want to hear what he had to say. I was ready to put this whole experience behind me, and focus on my sister and nephew.

Thankfully, her room wasn't too far off the front entrance of the medical center. I hurried into her room and let out the breath I'd been holding as soon as I saw her. She looked tired and her hair was damp, but she was alive.

"Abigail," she whispered as she opened her arms.

I hurried to her bed and pulled her into a hug. "Where did you go?"

When she didn't answer, I pulled back. I glanced down at her only to see that tears had filled her eyes.

"I'm so sorry, Abigail," she said, her voice barely a whisper.

"Ms. Orion?"

I glanced up to see a nurse had stepped into the room. I glanced back at Sabrina and then over to the nurse, a sick feeling forming in the pit of my stomach.

"Can I talk to you out in the hall?" the nurse asked.

I studied Sabrina for a moment before I leaned forward to kiss her cheek. "I'll be right back."

Sabrina nodded as she moved to grab a tissue from the box on the nightstand.

I followed the nurse out to the hallway, and she pulled Sabrina's door shut. Then she turned to face me.

"What happened to her?" I asked. I didn't want to

hear if it was bad news, but I was so exhausted from all of this that I couldn't stand the suspense.

The nurse crossed her arms. "How much do you know about postpartum depression?"

SWEET TEA &
SOUTHERN GENTLEMAN

I NORMALLY ENJOYED DRIVING in the more
remote parts of Harmony Island Inn property. I loved the
trees and the ocean view. But today, I couldn't bring
myself to enjoy any of it.

Shelby was still gone. In all honesty, I doubted that she
was even going to come back. In the picture that Tamara
had shown me, she looked so happy and content—something I hadn't seen on her face since she drove into town.

Which saddened me. I wanted to be enough for her. I
wanted her to love me like I'd always loved her—like I was
always going to love her.

But if staying and loving me made her that sad, I didn't
want that for her. Her past was such a train wreck, and she
deserved a bright future.

Even if I wasn't a part of that future.

I bounced on the gravel road as I pulled into the inn's driveway. I pulled the four-wheeler into its spot by the garage and killed the engine. Then I gathered up the plastic and ties from the flowers I'd bought and crumpled them in my hands as I climbed out of the seat and made my way across the driveway and up the back porch.

Tamara was in the kitchen, whipping up some cookies. Belle was standing on a step stool, mixing her own bowl of flour while Tamara scooped cookie rounds and plopped them on the cookie sheet.

I tossed the garbage in my hand into the nearby trash can and then hurried over to where Belle stood. I wrapped my arms around her and squeezed before I planted a kiss on her cheek.

"It smells amazing," I said as I glanced up at Tamara.

She smiled and nodded. "I found this recipe in Charlotte's book. Thought I'd make some." She paused, closed her eyes, and took in a deep breath. "And it smells like my memory of her." She glanced over at me and Belle. "Plus, munchkin here is helping."

Belle gave her a smile. I peered into her bowl and then back at my daughter. "Looks delicious." I spotted a fresh batch of cookies that were cooling on the counter and zeroed in on it. Tamara made a huffing noise, but she didn't say anything. Instead, she shot me a narrowed look before returning to the bowl of dough.

"Was your errand successful?" she asked.

I nodded, my mouth full of warm, gooey chocolate chip cookie. "Yep," I mumbled.

She glanced over at me. I could tell that she had questions for me, but I wasn't ready to tell anyone. It was private. Between me and, at one point, Charlotte. But she was gone, so now it was really just a place I went alone.

"Belle and I went to Godwin's this morning to get chocolate chips," Tamara said, waving her cookie scoop in my direction.

I quirked an eyebrow. "Really? How did that go?"

She shrugged. "Betty looked surprised when she saw me. And when it registered who I was with, I swear I thought she was going to call the sheriff." She met my gaze. "I guess you haven't told a lot of people that I'm back?"

I was mid-chew, so I just shrugged. "I figured that was your story to tell."

Tamara watched me for a moment but then sighed. "Yeah, you're right." She scooped another dollop of cookie dough onto the sheet. "Anyway, I guess Shelby's back."

My entire body went numb. For a split second, I doubted that she'd actually said Shelby's name. I was so far gone, when it came to missing Shelby, that I was hearing her voice or someone calling her name when I was completely alone.

I whipped my gaze to meet Tamara's, and she had a knowing look in her eyes. It took me a second to get my bearings, but I finally calmed down enough to take another bite and shrug. "Why would I care if she was back?"

Tamara shook her head. "Miles..."

I studied her. "What?"

She scooped some more dough onto the sheet and then glanced up at me. "Why are you lying to yourself? You care that she's back. You care that she left. You care that she moved out of the cottage." She sighed as she rested her hip against the counter and watched me.

I felt as if I were melting under her gaze. I wanted to brush off her words and tell her that she was lying. But it would be in vain. She knew she was speaking the truth, and deep down, I knew that as well.

I shook my head. "She walked away. What does it matter what I want?"

Tamara raised an eyebrow. "So that's how you're going to play it?"

Her question startled me. "How else am I supposed to 'play' it?" I used air quotes around the word, *play*.

"You have loved that girl from before you even met me. You loved her through our relationship. And even now, you love her more than anything. Maybe it's time you allow yourself to love her." She quirked an eyebrow. This was a one-eighty from a few nights ago when she'd asked me if I could see us getting back together.

She must have sensed my confusion because she shrugged and turned her focus back to the cookies. "There was a minute there when I thought we could pick up where we left off." Her gaze drifted over to Belle. "I want the best life for our daughter." She closed her lips as she paused. Then she sighed and turned back to me. "But I don't think that means marrying you while you are in love with another."

I frowned as I studied her. There was truth to her words, but she was forgetting one very important detail.

I turned away from Tamara, pushing my hands through my hair as I tipped my head back. "She doesn't want me, Tamara. And now, neither do you." I cursed under my breath. I was destined to be alone. That was what fate wanted me to know.

Tamara laughed. It was soft and sweet. "Miles, that girl wants you so bad."

My body stiffened. I turned to see Tamara shake her head.

"She would do anything for you and this is proof." She motioned between Belle and me. "The ultimate sacrifice. Loving someone enough to give up your happiness...that's what she did."

My emotions clung to my throat, making it hard to swallow. I'd tried to suppress my feelings for Shelby since she walked out on me, but a few words from Tamara and they were back, wreaking havoc on my insides.

"So what do I do?"

Tamara shrugged as she moved back to scooping cookie dough onto the sheet. "I love you because you're the father of my daughter, but I don't want to be your cupid. You got that girl to fall in love with you once. I'm sure you can do it again." Her hair fell in front of her face as she turned to look at me. I could see her gaze through the curtain and I could feel her affection for me.

It was what we would always feel for each other because of Belle. I wanted what was best for Tamara, but I wasn't ever going to want *her*. And that was okay. It was what she wanted as well. We'd made a mistake in the past, and that mistake created the beautiful human who was currently mixing her flour so hard, that puffs of it were rising over the rim of the bowl.

But that didn't mean we needed to keep making mistakes. Belle would always be happy because she had two parents who loved her—even if we weren't in love with each other.

"If it were you, what would you want?" I asked.

Tamara tossed her hair from her face so she could look at me head-on. She narrowed her eyes for a moment before she sighed. "Honestly?"

I nodded.

"You're not going to like it."

I shrugged. "Tell me."

She stopped scooping and set her hands down on the counter. "You have to wait. Wait for her to realize how much you mean to her."

"Wait?" I felt like all I'd ever done was wait. I was

tired and ready to move forward in my life. "What if..." My voice drifted off as the words refused to come out.

"What if what?"

I dropped my gaze to the floor for a moment. "What if she never comes back?"

When Tamara didn't speak, I raised my gaze up to see her studying me. Her smile was soft and her gaze understanding. "Then it was never meant to be. And you'll move on. You will."

I shoved my hands into my front pockets and nodded. "Yeah."

Silence fell between us. She knew what she said had hurt me, but I didn't blame her. It was good to think realistically. Shelby had spent most of her life avoiding this inn. It wasn't like she was knocking down the door to come back.

I needed to keep my expectations in check.

Needing something to do, I sighed and gave Tamara a smile. "I'm going to go chop some wood or something."

She nodded as she motioned to the cookies and the thin layer of flour dust that had coated most of the countertop. "I'll take care of this."

I didn't stop as I crossed the kitchen and headed down the back steps. I wasn't sure what I was going to do, all I knew was I needed to work off my frustration. Every cell in my body wanted to get in my truck and head down to The Shop Around the Corner and take Shelby in my arms and never let her go.

But Tamara was right. That was what *I* wanted. If I loved Shelby, I'd let her take her time. Even if it was killing me inside, I'd wait.

It was the one thing I could give her right now and, damn it, I was going to give it to her.

18

SHELBY

I MANAGED to find a red-eye flight from Vermont to North Carolina, and I got back to Abigail's apartment at three in the morning. I was confused by how silent the apartment was, but I shot her off a quick text before crashing on the couch.

When I woke up the next morning, I saw she'd replied. She needed me to open the bookstore because she'd stayed overnight at the medical center with Sabrina and Samuel. She didn't give more details, and I didn't push her. I figured that she would fill me in when she got back, so I sent her a thumbs-up after she texted where I could find the key for the shop.

I stopped by Godwin's, and almost had my heart ripped out when I saw Tamara climb out of Miles' truck and get Belle out of her car seat. They looked so perfect, mother and daughter. I stupidly walked into a sidewalk sign, knocking it over and drawing the attention of everyone in the parking lot.

Tamara glanced over at me, and all I could do was offer her a quick wave before slipping into my car and squelching the tears that threatened to spill.

I was done crying over Miles. I was happy for him...I was going to be happy for him. I loved Belle, and I was going to do what I could to keep her happy. Even if that meant sacrificing my own happiness.

When I got to the shop, I welcomed the relaxation that came from the mindless tasks I'd learned from Abigail. I got the coffee ready, stocked the front glass case, and swept the shop before I flipped the closed sign to open.

There was a steady stream of construction workers that flowed in and out of the shop, and in between the rushes, I got started with that day's baking list.

The front door opened for the umpteenth time just as I was wiggling the spatula under the last steaming-hot lemon poppyseed scone before setting it on the cooling rack. I wiped my hands on my apron and turned to the register with a smile on my face.

An older man ordered a coffee and chocolate chip cookie to go. I punched in his order as he handed me a twenty. I gave him his change and then waved for him to go to the end of the counter while I gathered his order.

I remained at that pace for the next thirty minutes as the flow of traffic continued for the second time that morning. My cheeks were warm and my body exhausted when the last construction worker took his order, bid me farewell, and headed out of the shop.

Now alone, I blew out my breath as I crossed my arms and leaned back against the counter. "This is getting insane," I said to myself as I reached behind me to grab my water bottle.

I'd only been able to take a few sips before the bells chimed on the door, marking a new customer. I replaced the cap of my water bottle and set it back where I'd stashed it. "Coming," I called out as I wiped my hands on the towel hanging next to me and turned.

My entire body froze. Miles was standing in front of the counter with his hands in his pockets. His gaze was dark as he met mine.

It took a moment for the shock to wear off. Thankfully, instinct took over as I focused on my job. "What can I get you?" I asked as I forced my attention to the cash register and waited for his response.

"Shelby."

His voice was deep and sent shivers down my spine. I stared at the numbers in front of me, hating the fact that my entire body responded to his voice. Was I ever going to get over him? Was I ever going to be happy?

"What can I get you?" I asked again, praying that he would just move on instead of staring at me.

"Shelby, I—"

"The lemon scones are fresh baked this morning," I said as I waved toward the glass case next to me. "And if you haven't had our lattes, they are to die for." I paused, waiting to see if that would encourage him to place an order.

Instead, the silence around us felt like the entire world screaming at me. Why wasn't he talking? Why was he here? What did he want from me? I'd promised Titan that I would talk to Miles if given the chance, but this didn't feel like that chance. Not after I saw Tamara and Belle at Godwin's. They looked like a family. I couldn't break that up.

"I'm sorry," he whispered, his voice so deep that it sent shivers down my spine.

I couldn't keep my gaze away from him any longer. He'd stepped closer to the counter now and was studying me.

"What do you want from me, Miles?" I winced as my voice broke. There was so much pain in his gaze, and my first instinct was to take it all away...but I couldn't put myself out there like that.

"I was worried about you. I..." He winced. "I should have come after you, but I wasn't sure how you would take it, and I wanted to give you time. I just didn't think you'd run..." His voice dropped, and he studied me like he wasn't sure if he should continue.

I wasn't ready for this conversation, so I just nodded, determined to take it in a different direction. "I appreciate you staying away. It's for the best." I raised my gaze to meet his. "For everyone."

He winced again like I'd just slapped him in the face. He parted his lips like he wanted to say more, but there was no way I wanted to hear it, so I pulled a wax paper sheet from the box on the counter and slid open the door to the glass case.

"How's Belle?" I asked as I grabbed a scone and shook open a paper bag with the shop's logo printed on the front of it.

"She's good."

I nodded, keeping my focus on gathering food. He hadn't ordered, but I was impatient to get him out of the shop, so I was going to put a plethora of choices together and send him on his way.

"That's good." I paused as a smile emerged on my lips. "I miss that little girl."

Miles went silent. I could see him from the corner of my eye as he shifted his weight. "She misses you, too...a lot." His voice dropped an octave with the last word, and the sound sent shivers down my spine.

My entire body stopped moving as I let his words wash over me. I knew we were talking about Belle, but there was a part of me that hoped his words meant something more.

"How's Tamara?" I needed to remember why we couldn't be together. I'd walked out on him so he could be a family with the mother of his daughter.

"She's good."

His words felt like a dagger to my chest. I winced as

anger built up inside of me. But then I pushed my emotions back down. It was good that Tamara was doing well. My beef wasn't with her. It was with fate for thinking it was so funny to keep torturing me like this.

"How was...Vermont?"

I whipped my gaze up to meet his. He was studying me with a pain so intense that I couldn't breathe.

"How did you know?"

He scoffed as he pushed his hand through his hair. "So you're not denying it."

My lips parted but nothing came out. I wanted to say that being with Titan meant nothing. That all I could think about when I was away was how much I wanted to be here. In his arms. In his bed. I needed him like I needed air. But that wouldn't be fair.

Not when I'd told him that he needed to stay away. That he needed to fall in love with Tamara. That I was never going to love him like he wanted me to, so we needed to stop while we were ahead.

"It was good," I finally managed out. I swallowed, a lump forming in my throat and making it impossible for me to keep my composure.

Miles kept his gaze focused on me as if he were waiting for me to break. I squared my shoulders and lifted the bag that was now stuffed with pastries.

"On the house," I said as I held it out for him to take.

"I didn't—"

"Just take them," I pleaded with him.

Miles stared at me for a moment before he reached out and grabbed the bottom of the bag. We stood there in silence. He didn't drop his gaze and neither did I.

It was as if we were daring the other person to speak first. The tension in the air was palpable and caused my heart to race. But I wasn't going to break. This was for his own good. He needed to be with Tamara, and that was it.

I wasn't going to take any other answer.

Titan didn't know what he was talking about. His relationship with Samantha was not the same as my relationship with Miles. There were more hearts and lives at stake in our situation.

Miles coming to the shop wasn't a sign from fate. It was just a regular occurrence I was going to have to get used to. He lived in this town, and for the next six months, I was going to have to be in this town as well.

It was time we acted like adults and moved on.

"Thanks for stopping by," I said as I forced a smile.

Miles just stared at me. His brows were knit together, and I could tell he had so many thoughts storming in his gaze. But I didn't want to hear it. I nodded toward the door.

"If that's all, you can leave." The last few words came out barely a whisper. I waited to see what he was going to do.

I didn't want him to leave, and yet, I wanted him to make it easier for me by leaving first. I needed him to stay away from me, because my strength to stay away from him was waning.

He needed to leave before I said something stupid.

"That's all?" he asked.

I nodded. "That's all."

He stared at me for a moment longer before he crumpled the top part of the bag and turned. He paused for a split second in front of the door but then pushed through and disappeared around the corner of the building.

I collapsed against the counter, my arms hugging my stomach as my heart broke into a million pieces. That was our first interaction since I got back, and even though I felt like I was dying, I'd survived it.

Now, I just needed time to pass so my heart would start to heal.

19

SHELBY

SWEET TEA &
SOUTHERN GENTLEMAN

THANKFULLY, Fanny showed up at five to take over. I was exhausted and ready to crawl into bed and bawl my eyes out. Miles never came back, and I spent the rest of the day jumping every time the door opened. I'd hoped and dreaded that he was coming back.

It was like living in my own hell.

I gave Fanny the rundown for the day and then grabbed my purse and headed out to my car. The clouds above looked ominous as they gathered above me. I could feel the rain that threatened to fall.

Once I pulled into Abigail's building, I turned off my car and hurried inside. Just as I unlocked the door, I heard laughing from the living room. I stuffed my keys into my purse and set it down on the kitchen counter before rounding the corner to see Abigail standing in the living room with an older gentleman and a woman with perfectly styled grey hair.

"Shelby!" Abigail exclaimed when she saw me. She crossed the space between us and wrapped her arms around me. "Meet my dad, Spencer, and his new wife, Penny."

I let her lead me over to them. They each shook my hand while giving me exhausted, yet relieved, smiles.

"It's nice to meet you, Shelby," Spencer said as he wrapped his arm around Abigail's shoulders. "Abi's been telling me how you've been helping out around here."

I gave Abigail a weak smile. "She's really been helping me."

Spencer glanced between Abigail and me a few times.

"Sounds like you were each other's life rafts," Penny said as she gave me a soft smile.

"I guess you could say that," I replied. Then I pulled at my jeans and t-shirt. "I'm a mess. I'm going to jump into the shower if you don't mind."

They all nodded, and I hurried to Abigail's room to grab my stuff. Sabrina's door was shut, and I wondered for a moment if she was in there. But then I brushed that thought away as I gathered my stuff up for a shower and disappeared into the bathroom.

I felt more alive once I stepped out of the shower and slipped on a simple summer dress. I let my hair air dry as I applied a bit of makeup—just to feel alive—and headed out to the living room. When I found it empty, I investigated Samuel's room before finding Abigail lying on her bed.

"Where did everyone go?" I asked as I moved to join her.

"My dad and Penny got a room at the Apple Blossom B&B. They drove through the night to get here, so they are exhausted."

I turned to look at her. "What happened? Why did they drive here?"

She sat up and worry flashed alongside relief on her face. "I got home yesterday to find Sabrina and Samuel were gone."

I frowned. "Where did they go?"

I let her talk. She told me about feeling exhausted from work and coming home to find Sabrina and Samuel gone. She told me about calling the police and how they brushed aside her concerns. I moved to sit next to her as she told me about how Anders was drunk and couldn't help her and how it had been Bash who'd come to her rescue.

Then she told about the hospital and staying the night by Sabrina's side, crying into the comforter because she felt like she'd failed her sister. I rested my hand on hers as she nodded and wiped away a tear that had slid down her cheek. But that only lasted a moment before she smiled over at me.

"But she's back home and the doctor gave us medication.

I'm hopeful that I'll start seeing my sister back to her normal, happy self." She pushed herself up with her hand until she was leaning against the headboard. "It's been a long 24 hours." She sniffled as she shifted her focus to me. "What about you? What about Titan? What happened there?"

I sighed and settled back against the pillows next to her. When I told her about Gran's journal that she'd snuck in, she gave me a sly smile.

"So it worked?"

I nodded. "It worked." Then I paused. "I mean, it doesn't solve everything, but it helped put me on the right path. Helped me realize that I needed to stop running and figure my life out here in Harmony."

Abigail cheered as she turned so she could hug me. "I'm so happy for you." Then she pulled back. "So did you see it?"

I frowned. "See what?"

She studied me. "The passage about Miles and the..." She raised her eyebrows as she moved her head like she expected me to finish her sentence.

"And the...what?"

Her eyes narrowed. "Did you really not read it?"

I stood and crossed the room to my suitcase, where I pulled the journal out. "I only got about halfway," I said as I tossed it to her.

She caught it and started flipping through the pages. I watched her, confused by what she was trying to hint at.

Suddenly, she pumped her hand in triumph and handed the journal over to me. "Here. Right here."

I leaned over and took the journal from her.

"Dear Shelby," I started out. "Today, Miles showed me the gravestone he bought for your..." the next word caught in my throat. I blinked a few times, reading the four-letter word over and over again.

"Baby," I whispered at the same time as Abigail.

I glanced up at her. "He bought a gravestone for my baby?"

Abigail pinched her lips together and nodded. "He bought a gravestone for your baby."

I shook my head as I read the sentence over again. "Why would he do that?"

Abigail took the journal from me and continued reading where I'd left off. "He vowed to me that he would place fresh flowers on the grave every month. He took me and Belle out this morning to see. It was at the same spot we found behind the inn years ago and picnicked at." Abigail glanced up at me before she dropped her gaze to the journal and continued. "That boy really does love you." Abigail's voice softened as my grandmother's words lingered in the air.

My entire body was numb. My heart was pounding so hard that I could hear it in my ears. I wanted to believe it, but at the same time, I didn't. How could Miles love me so much that he would build a memorial for the child I'd lost?

"Do you think it's true?" I asked as I glanced up at Abigail.

She shrugged. "Do you think it's true?"

I chewed on my lip. I had to know. I had to know right now. "I'm going to be back," I said as I started walking backwards out of the room.

"Shelby, wait," Abigail followed after me. She grabbed my arm. "I can't go with you. I can't leave Sabrina here alone."

I pulled my hand away. Nothing was going to keep me here. Nothing. I had to see if this was true. If Miles loved me enough to do this.

"I'll be fine. I know where to go. I know the spot." I grabbed my purse from the counter and slipped on my shoes. "I'll be just fine," I repeated, hoping to ease the worry written all over Abigail's face.

I grabbed the door handle and turned, shutting the door on Abigail before she could try to keep me here. I hurried down the stairs and over to my car where I stuck the key into the ignition. There was a low rumble and it took a few tries, but the engine finally roared to life.

I praised the heavens as I pulled out of the parking spot and sped down the street. It took me about fifteen minutes to reach the hidden dirt road on the outskirts of Harmony Inn. Brush hit the sides of the car as I went deeper into the woods. Rain was starting to fall, fulfilling the promise of moisture that the sky had hinted at before.

I turned on the windshield wipers as I continued

through to the spot that Gran, Miles, and I had found years ago. Normally, we would ride the four-wheeler to the spot, but I couldn't borrow the one at the inn. Miles would know I was here.

Suddenly, there was a break in the brush, and a huge opening spread out in front of me. Even though it was getting dark, I knew that the ocean wasn't too far off.

I pushed the car into park and pulled open the door. Rain hit my hair and face as I stepped out of the car. I knew it was only a matter of time before I was soaked to the bone, but I didn't care. I needed to see.

I pushed my feet against the sand as I walked to the dune that overlooked the ocean. The one Gran would spread a blanket over and feed us peanut butter and home-made-jam sandwiches. We'd eat and laugh and go swimming in the ocean afterward.

Through the soft glow of my headlights, I saw it. It was small and stood out of the ground only a foot or so. But it was there. A gravestone.

I walked to it, not feeling any of the rain that was beating down on me. Once I was in front of it, I dropped to my knees.

Baby Sorenson

If you only knew how loved you were before you left us.

I sobbed as I knelt in front of it. I reached out and ran my fingers across the engraving. There was so much hurt and pain wrapped up in my past. In the loss of my baby. In the loss of my childhood. In the loss of my mother.

I'd held onto that pain for so long that I didn't know who I was anymore. Or who I could be without it. I was in this sort of limbo hell, and I was tired.

I closed my eyes and let my tears mix with the rain that ran down my skin.

And I just cried.

I cried for myself, for my child, and for my grandmother. I cried for the pain that I'd held onto for so long. I cried for the relationships I would never be able to fix with my mother or my grandmother and for the baby I was never going to hold.

Everyone was gone. I was the only left, trying to piece together the parts of our family that were so broken. I feared I was so broken that the parts of me affected by my past would never come together again. That I would never love or feel loved. I was a shell of a person just moving through space and time.

And then I cried for Miles and all the pain I'd put him through. He'd loved me so hard for so long, and I never allowed myself to love him back in the same way. He wanted me. He wanted me to be there for Belle.

He wanted me as his wife. And I'd pushed him away.

I pulled out my phone, my hands shaking as I stared down at the screen. I swiped it on, taking note that I barely had any bars. I gathered my courage as I opened our text message chain and began to type.

Me: I'm so sorry I hurt you. I shouldn't have walked away. Will you ever forgive me?

I stared down at my text, the rain running down my face and splashing onto my screen. I wanted to say more, but I wasn't sure if I should. Then I shook my head and pressed send. He had to know that I wasn't going to push him away anymore. Whatever he chose between Tamara and me, I was always going to be here for him.

I waited for the message to send, but it never did. I glanced to the top of my phone only to see that the meager bar that had been there a moment ago was gone. I sighed as I slipped my phone into my pocket and turned my focus back to the gravestone in front of me.

My gaze drifted over and I took in the flowers sitting in a small vase on the side. They looked fresh and...real. I leaned over and inhaled. The sweet smell of lilies filled my nose. I closed my eyes as a cleansing feeling washed over me.

It was as if all the pain that I'd held onto for so long... faded. Reading my grandmother's journal, going to Vermont and talking to Titan, returning home even though I never thought I would come back. All of these moments had led up to this one.

I was finally going to stop holding onto what I couldn't change in my past and focus on what I was going to do to change my future. To make my future a bright one. One where I was happy.

Thunder rumbled around me as I knelt on the ground. I glanced up to see a flash of lightning dance across the sky. I squinted as rain threatened to run into my eyes.

Realizing that it probably wasn't safe to be out here anymore, I pushed myself to standing. Just as I did, a loud crack sounded above my head.

Before I could react, a weight dropped on my head and I was thrown to the ground. I closed my eyes as pain seeped from the top of my head and radiated throughout my body.

It felt like a tree branch had been dropped on my head. My whole body ached as I lay there. Rain splashed on my skin but I was too stunned to move.

I moaned as I lifted my hand to the back of my head, and a warm, sticky liquid coated my fingers. My gaze was hazy as I peeked at it and saw bright-red blood. I closed my eyes and stilled my body. I needed to go, but the rest of me wasn't in a hurry to get out of here. For now, I was just going to lie here until I found the strength to move.

However long that took.

SWEET TEA &
SOUTHERN GENTLEMAN

THE RAIN FELT OMINOUS. I stood on the porch, staring out at the storm as it completely surrounded the inn. The wind whipped around me as darkness clouded the skies. It matched my mood. My mind wasn't settled at all. Something felt off, but I wasn't sure what it was.

The sound of the front door opening drew my attention over. Tamara pulled the door shut behind her before she pulled the blanket around her shoulders tighter. She had a steaming mug of tea in her other hand. When she saw me watching her, she smiled. "Hey."

I nodded before turning my attention back to the rain. "It's coming down hard."

She appeared next to me, holding her mug between both her hands. "It is." She sighed and took a sip. "Belle's sleeping."

I glanced over at her. "Thanks."

She smiled. "Of course."

I turned to face her head-on. "I really mean it. Thanks for coming back. I know it couldn't have been easy, but I'm glad you did. Belle really needs her mom."

Tears brimmed her eyes as she took another sip. "I just hope that I haven't ruined everything."

I shook my head. "Take it from someone who was disappointed by his parents, children will always love their mom and dad. No matter how many times they screw up." I shrugged as I shoved my hands into my front pockets. "It's just what we do."

Tamara didn't respond. Instead, she stared out at the rain, taking a sip every so often. "So are you going to talk to her?"

"Who?"

She glanced over at me. "Shelby."

My stomach knotted at the mention of her name. "Ah," I whispered. Then I pushed my hand through my hair. "I saw her in town today."

I felt Tamara's gaze on me, but she didn't say anything.

"I don't know what I thought she would say to me when I walked into the bookstore, but she basically gave me a bunch of pastries and sent me on my way." I shrugged. "So I don't know what to make of that."

Tamara was watching me from over the brim of her mug. I felt like she was dissecting my words. I distracted myself by pulling out my phone and swiping the screen on.

"So what are you going to do?" she asked, but I really didn't hear her. I was distracted by the fact that I had a text message...from Shelby.

"Hang on," I said as I pressed on the text bubble icon and brought up the message.

Shelby: I'm so sorry I hurt you. I shouldn't have walked away. Will you ever forgive me?

My entire body froze as I read her words once more. And then again. And again.

"What happened?" Tamara asked, her voice sounding panicked.

"Shelby," I whispered as I brought my phone up to show her.

Her gaze drifted back and forth as she read the text. Then, she turned her focus back to me. "What does that mean?"

My heart was pounding now. Did this mean what I wanted it to mean? "Do you think..." I wanted to say the words, but I didn't dare hope. Setting those words free into the world would do just that—give me hope that Shelby wanted me like I've always wanted her.

"Call her."

I froze as Tamara's words slammed into me. I glanced up to see her soft smile.

"Call her," she repeated.

"I should call her," I said, mostly for myself. I needed to force my body to act because my mind wasn't strong enough.

Tamara nodded before she took another sip.

I didn't allow myself to wait or to overthink what I needed to do. I pressed on the call button and brought my phone to my cheek before I lost my nerve. I waited, but the call never rang through. Instead, all I was met with was the sound of her voicemail.

I frowned as I hung up and dialed again...only to have the same thing happen again.

My stomach churned. It was a strange text, but now that I wasn't able to reach her, worst-case scenarios raced through my mind. So I did the only thing that made sense; I called Abigail.

Thankfully, the phone only rang twice before she picked up.

"Hello?"

"Abigail? It's Miles."

There was a pause. "Hey, Miles."

I cleared my throat as I began to pace. "Hey, I got a text from Shelby, and it was strange. When I went to call her back, it just went to voicemail. Is she with you?"

Another pause. "She's not here. She went out."

I blew out my breath as I tipped my face up. "This sounds crazy, but I have a bad feeling. Can you tell me where she went?"

"Um..."

I stopped moving as I waited. My stomach was doing somersaults now. Something was wrong. "Abigail?"

"She was reading her grandmother's journal, and she found the part about the gravestone."

I froze. She knew?

"So, I'm guessing she's there right now."

I peered out at the rain that was still coming down. "She's probably soaked."

"I wanted to go with her, but I couldn't leave my sister. You should probably go make sure she's okay."

Abigail's words sounded distant as I crossed the porch and pulled open the front door. "I'll be back," I tossed over my shoulder to Tamara as the door slammed shut behind me. Then I told Abigail I would look for Shelby and then promptly hung up.

After grabbing the keys to the four-wheeler, I grabbed a jacket and an umbrella just in case I needed it and headed out the back door. I jogged across the driveway and climbed onto the four-wheeler.

It felt like an eternity before I broke through the brush and into the opening where I'd set up a memorial for the baby she lost. Call it grief, call it wanting some control over what happened, but a few years ago, I purchased a gravestone and set it up in a place that had meant a lot to me and her.

I made a point to come out here at least once a month to place flowers on the grave. And when I needed time to think, I found myself feeling peace here. But now that Shelby knew what I'd done, I was scared that I'd overstepped.

Losing the baby had been her experience, not mine. And I didn't want her to think that I was holding onto something I didn't have a right to.

My gaze went right to the gravestone, and that's when my heart sank. A tree branch was lying on the ground, and after a closer look, I saw Shelby underneath it. Adrenaline coursed through my body as I crossed the space between us and lifted the branch.

"Shelby," I yelled against the wind and rain. I crouched down next to her, inspecting her body for movement.

She opened her eyes and looked confused. But as she studied me, recognition passed through her gaze. "Miles?"

She was alive. I didn't hesitate as I scooped her up into my arms and hugged her to my chest. I was going to get her back to the inn as fast as I could. She shivered, but didn't push me away as she snuggled into my arms. As soon as I got to the four-wheeler, I set her on the seat before wrapping the jacket around her shoulders. Then I climbed on behind her and pulled her against my chest as I started the engine.

"Hold onto me." I pressed my lips close to her ear so she could hear me.

She nodded, her body vibrating from her shivers.

I kept the pace as steady as I could, making sure to lift my arm up to push aside any low-hanging branch that I thought might touch her. It felt like an eternity before we got back to the inn. I pulled up right next to the back porch and killed the engine.

Shelby started to climb down, but I didn't let her. Instead, I scooped her up in my arms once more and took the porch stairs two at a time. She made a noise like she was going to protest, but I wasn't going to hear any of it. She was hurt and I wasn't going to stop until I knew she was safe.

Thankfully, Tamara wasn't in the kitchen when I entered. I kicked off my shoes before shutting the door behind us. Then I crossed the kitchen to the hallway and didn't stop until I was in my room. I set Shelby down and then turned and shut my bedroom door.

When I turned back around, I saw Shelby standing there, shivering. Her eyes were wide as she stared at me. I was done with the games we were playing. I was made to love her, and I wasn't going to let her leave until she knew that.

"Take off your dress," I demanded, my voice low.

She frowned. "What?"

I pushed my hand through my hair, spraying water everywhere. "Take off your dress," I repeated.

"Miles, I—"

"I need to see that you're okay." I closed my eyes for a moment as fear coated my chest. Fear that something might have happened to Shelby when I wasn't there to protect her. Fear that she hated me for creating the memorial. Fear that this was the only chance I was going to get to make sure she knew she was the only person who mattered to me after Belle.

When she didn't answer, I peeked over at her. Maybe she was worried that I was going to ask her to stay. So I added, "I promise, after this, I'll leave you alone for good."

She studied me. When our gazes met, I couldn't understand the turmoil that raced through her eyes. She didn't break the connection before she sighed and began to pull the bottom of her dress up.

In one swift movement, she pulled her dress over her head. I sucked in my breath as I studied her. She was wearing a black bra and panties, but I wasn't focused there. I was too busy dragging my gaze over her skin, desperate to see that she wasn't hurt.

That she was okay.

"I'm fine, Miles. Really," she whispered, her voice catching on each shiver that rocked through her body.

I knew she was cold, I just had to make sure she was okay. I crossed the space between us and started to circle around her body, scanning every inch of her skin for bruises or cuts. Shelby held still, her breathing soft and shallow. I could feel her gaze on me as she watched me walk around her.

When I came to the front, I stepped closer to her. Her gaze was on my chest as I stared down at her. I needed her to look up. I needed her to see that no matter what she said to me in this moment, I was going to love her until the day I died.

I wanted no one else...I just wanted her.

Slowly, Shelby brought her gaze up to mine. My heart pounded in my chest as she searched my eyes. I could see all her questions, and I wanted to answer them. I wanted to calm her down. I wanted her to seem as happy with me as she was with Titan.

"Why did you do that?" she finally whispered.

I frowned. "Do what?"

She shivered, and I stepped closer, aching to reach out and touch her. To pull her to my chest and hold her until she was warm.

"Why did you get a gravestone for my baby?"

I reached out, my fingers a hair's breadth away from her. I wanted to touch her, but I didn't want to overstep. So my fingertips lingered ever so close to her skin.

"I needed to feel close to you. I wanted you to have a memorial place for your baby. I wanted to tell you. I just didn't know how. And Charlotte, she wanted me to wait to say anything to you. She wanted you to come down here on your own, and she feared that if I told you, it would be a reason for you to stay away."

Tears filled Shelby's eyes as she studied me. She chewed on her bottom lip as she took in my words. My gaze drifted to her mouth, and all I wanted was to feel them against my own. The kiss we'd shared in my bathroom haunted me.

"But why did you do it?"

I frowned. "What do you mean?"

"Why did you do that for me? No one has ever cared enough about me or my pain to do something like that. Why did you?"

I held her gaze as I wondered if she was joking. She had to know. She had to know that I loved her. I'd told her that. "Shelby, I love you," I said, my voice rumbling in my chest from the emotions that coated my words. "I will always love you." I closed the distance between us, my fingers wrapping around her shoulder. The warmth and softness of her skin shocked my body, and it was talking all of my strength not to pull her to me.

"I know you want me to make things work with Tamara..." I blew out my breath as Shelby's gaze made its way to me. There was a vulnerable look in her gaze that made my heart pound harder. I wanted to give her the world. I wanted to love Tamara because Shelby wanted me to.

But I didn't. And I was never going to love her that way. And I didn't think it was fair to lead Tamara on and have her believe that ours was a relationship worth saving.

Because I loved Shelby. I was *always* going to love her.

"But I can't. And it's not fair to ask her to settle for a man whose heart is with another woman." I dipped down to catch Shelby's gaze once more. "My heart is with you. It will always be with you. And I'm willing to wait. I'm willing to let you take the time you need. I'm willing"—my heart squeezed at these words, but I knew I needed to say them—"to stand aside if you want to love another man. But for me and what I want..." I ran my thumb over her skin and felt goosebumps rise up from my touch.

"I want you. Forever."

A tear slid down Shelby's cheek. She sucked in her breath, a sob escaping her lips. Suddenly, her arms were around my neck as her body crashed into mine. It took me a moment to understand what was happening, but when she buried her face into my chest, instinct took over.

I wrapped my arms around her back and squeezed her as tightly as I could. I feared that if I didn't hold onto her, she was going to slip away once more.

"I'm so sorry," she cried, her voice muffled by my shirt.

I shook my head as I reached up and held her head to my chest. "Shh," I said, closing my eyes. "You have nothing to be sorry for."

She paused before she pulled back. "You shouldn't love me. I'm not worth it."

I moved my hand from the back of her head to her cheek and cradled her face in my palm. "You are worth the moon." My gaze drifted to her lips, and I held back for a moment before I dipped down and brushed my lips against hers. Electricity zapped through my body as I allowed the kiss to linger. "You are everything I've ever wanted," I murmured against her lips.

Shelby's hands made their way to my neck as she pulled me to her. She deepened the kiss, her lips parting as she let me in. My hand roamed over her back, her shoulders, and my fingers traced the outline of her bra.

She sucked in her breath when I slipped my hand under the strap and pulled her to my chest. Her kisses turned desperate, like she wanted me as much as I wanted her.

"Miles," she murmured as her hands slipped from my neck to my shoulders and then my chest.

My shirt was still soaking wet, so I leaned back long enough to pull it off. Her hands splayed across my chest, the warmth of her palms burning my skin.

I wanted so much in this moment. I wanted to show Shelby how much I loved her. I wanted her to wrap her body around mine. I wanted to hear her gasp my name as I pleased her all night long.

But I couldn't. I made a vow to Belle that I wasn't going to play with fate again. The next woman I would be physical with, would be my wife.

I growled and pulled back, my entire body aching to stay close to Shelby. My resolve waning with every stroke of her tongue on my own or the feeling of her hands slipping down my abs and hovering right above my jeans.

I wanted to explore her, but I knew if I kept at it, I wouldn't have the strength to walk away. If I was going to stop, it had to be now.

"Go take a shower," I commanded as I pointed toward my bathroom.

Shelby's eyes were hazy and her lips swollen. She looked startled and upset that I'd stepped away. "What?"

I took another step back. "If I keep going, I won't stop." My gaze turned pleading. "Go take a shower."

Shelby studied me for a moment before she pinched her lips together and nodded. "Okay."

She started to turn, but I couldn't let her go thinking that I didn't want this. So I reached out and grabbed her elbow. "It's not that I don't want you." My thumb stroked her skin. "I want you more than you will ever know. I just...can't. Not until you have my ring on your finger and I have yours on mine."

Her eyes widened. Fear rushed through me. Maybe I'd read this all wrong. Maybe she didn't want that with me. I needed to save this. "Not that I'm asking. I understand that you might want something different."

Shelby paused as if she were trying to digest my words, but then, she stepped forward with a determined look in her eye. She placed her hands on my chest and slowly dragged them up until she wrapped her fingers in my hair and rose up onto her tiptoes. Her lips found mine, and she kissed me so hard, so passionately, that I felt as if I were sinking into her body.

"I love you," she whispered when she finally broke the kiss and pulled back.

My entire body froze as those three little words left her lips. The three little words that I'd been aching to hear. That I'd been desperate to hear.

"I love you, Miles," she repeated as she held my gaze. "I'd marry you tomorrow."

I clenched my jaw. My ability to stay away from her was teetering on the cliff. If she didn't step away now, it was going to disappear forever. "Go shower," I growled. "Now."

Shelby stepped back, chewing her lip as she stared at me. I clenched my fist, forcing myself to focus on my promises to my daughter as they clashed with the molten hot desire that was coursing through my veins.

Shelby would shower here, and I was going to find a vacant room and shower there. Hopefully, afterward, I could find the strength to keep my hands off of her long enough to figure out what I was going to do.

When the bathroom door was shut and Shelby was out of sight, I let out my breath. I grabbed some fresh clothes, left a set out for Shelby to wear, and hurried off to the only vacant room in the inn. I shut the door behind me and proceeded to take the coldest shower I'd ever taken.

While I was in there, the path I needed to take became clear. I knew what I was going to do, and there was no question in my mind what was going to make me happy.

I was going to marry Shelby as soon as I could.

She would be my wife, and I was never ever going to let her go.

21

SHELBY

SWEET TEA &
SOUTHERN GENTLEMAN

LAST NIGHT, I didn't bother to go back to Abigail's house. Instead, I texted her, letting her know that I was staying at the inn, and she responded with a celebrating emoji. I shook my head. But thoughts of Abigail were quickly forgotten as Miles and I spent the night holding each other and talking about our past.

We laughed at the memories we held together. But eventually, the laughter died down and we just lay there holding each other. Miles pressed his lips to the top of my head and repeated over and over that he loved me.

I rose up onto my elbow, met his gaze, and told him that I loved him back. I could see the affection and desire for me in his gaze as his fingers threaded through my hair and he guided my lips to his. We kissed until the heat between us became too much and he growled and pulled back. I wanted so much to be with him in that moment, but I respected his decision, so I snuggled into the crook of his arm, using his chest as my pillow. We lay there in silence until my eyes grew heavy and I fell asleep.

I woke up to the sunlight breaking through the curtains and spilling onto the bed. I yawned and stretched, wiggling my body in an effort to wake up. I glanced over to see that Miles was still lying on his back with his head tipped to the side. I giggled softly as I studied him. His dark eyelashes splayed across his cheeks, and he looked so content.

Not wanting to wake him up, I snuggled back under his arm and rested my hand on his chest. I watched as my hand rose and fell with each breath he took. He was warm and comfortable, and he felt like...home.

Heat burned in my stomach, and my heart began to pound as I closed my eyes and allowed myself to feel. I was in love with Miles. Thinking back to growing up, it felt like this was a sentiment I'd held for a while, but I hadn't been self-aware enough to label those feelings.

I'd always known that he would be there for me. And in a way, I wondered if his feelings for me were what had drawn me to him. Regardless, Miles and I were meant for each other.

Our parents brought us together as kids, but fate was what kept us together. I was meant to love him and he was meant to love me.

My stomach growled as I lay there. I winced and

glanced up, expecting to see Miles stir, but he didn't. Instead, he lay there, completely asleep.

I slowly pulled away from him until I slipped off the bed and stood. Miles grunted but didn't move. I found his robe and wrapped it around my body as I padded out of his room and down the hall.

I heard a woman's soft voice coming from the kitchen, which caused me to slow. I hadn't seen Tamara since I'd gotten back, and I wasn't sure how she was going to react if I walked into the kitchen. Especially when it was apparent that I'd stayed the night in Miles' room.

I sucked in my breath and headed into the kitchen. Tamara was standing at the counter with Belle, whose eyes widened when she saw me. I smiled at the sight of the little girl who'd wormed her way into my heart and set up camp.

"Belle!" I exclaimed as she climbed down from the stool she was standing on and hurried over to me.

I wrapped my arms around her and pulled her up. She squealed and threw her arms around my neck. Tears pricked my eyes as I held her, never wanting to let her go again.

After about a minute of embrace, Belle began to wiggle and press against my shoulders. I kissed her on the top of her head before setting her down. She padded back over to Tamara, who had been watching us. I couldn't read her gaze, so I offered her a soft smile when I noticed her appraising Miles' robe.

"Hey," I said, not sure what to do other than stand there awkwardly.

Tamara's gaze met mine, and she held it for a moment before a smile crept across her lips. "I'm glad you're safe."

I frowned. "I wasn't safe?"

Tamara nodded as she set Belle up with some crayons and paper before making her way over to the coffee pot and pulling down two mugs. "Miles was really worried about you last night."

"Oh."

Silence filled the kitchen. The awkwardness felt so thick that I could cut it with a knife. I wasn't sure where she and Miles had landed, and I hated that I'd pushed them together only to walk back in here and take him away from her.

Tamara filled the mugs with coffee and then walked back over to me, handing me one. I thanked her, and we stood next to each other, sipping in silence. Then she cleared her throat and set down her mug before turning to face me.

She stared at me for a moment, and my breath held in my throat as I waited for her to say something...to scream at me...or smack me across the face. My entire body tensed as time ticked by.

She sighed and a slow smile spread across her lips. "Thanks, Shelby."

I'd expected a lot of things, I hadn't expected that.

"What?" I asked before I could stop the word from leaving my lips.

She reached forward, and I tensed, anticipating a blow. Instead, she wrapped her arms around my shoulders and pulled me closer. "Thanks for wanting something more for my daughter. For fighting to keep Miles and me together." She dropped her arms and stepped back, meeting my gaze once more. "It was really a selfless thing you did." She gave me a weak smile. "But Miles and I aren't meant to be together. I deserve someone who loves me. And Miles..." Her voice drifted off as her gaze shifted to Belle and then back to me. "Miles loves you."

My cheeks heated at her words as butterflies erupted in my stomach. I pinched my lips together and nodded. "Yeah, I know."

Her smile was sad but encouraging. "I just hope that you're sticking around for good now. I had to live with him over the last week, and he was miserable without you around." She picked up her coffee and took another sip. "You're planning on staying, right?" Her gaze drifted over to Belle. "Miles and I have a daughter to raise, and..." Her voice trailed off as she glanced over at me. "I'd love for her to have you in her life as well."

The tears began to flow as I nodded. "I want the same thing too."

Tamara's eyes filled with tears as well, but she kept them from falling. Instead, she cleared her throat, gave me a smile and a nod, and then turned her attention to the fridge and pulled out the eggs. "Breakfast won't cook itself," she whispered, emotions coating her words like they were coating my throat.

Wanting a moment to compose myself, and giving the same grace to Tamara, I grabbed my coffee mug, kissed Belle on the top of her head, and hurried out of the kitchen and into the living room. My pace slowed as I glanced around.

It had been so long since I'd been in this part of the inn. I'd spent most of my time here avoiding this place—avoiding my memories. Now, they still hurt, but facing them felt like something I could do.

I hated that I hadn't been here for the last moments of my grandmother's life, but I knew I hadn't been ready to face what had happened. It was sad that she died without rekindling our relationship, but I hoped wherever she was now, she knew that I'd forgiven her.

"I'm going to be okay," I whispered to the familiar portraits that hung on the wall.

I wasn't sure how long I spent wandering the halls. Most of the guests were out, thankfully. So I wasn't bothering anyone as I paced back and forth. When I finally came to the room where the horrible night had taken place, I stopped and stared at the familiar oak door.

This was the room where the miscarriage had started.

The night that changed my life forever.

I stood there, remembering the pain and fear. I remembered my grandmother rushing in and out of the room while she was on the phone with the ambulance. I remembered Miles standing in the shadows, a hollow expression on his face like he wanted to do something but didn't know what.

I remembered crying out for Clint, knowing that he'd left me but not really accepting it.

My whole life was turned upside-down. All of the pain that I'd felt from my mother leaving and dying in a car crash added to this. I broke. I broke and I never thought I would be put back together again.

"Shelby." Miles' soft whisper was followed by the feeling of his arms wrapping around me. He pulled me to his chest as a sob escaped my lips. "I'm so sorry."

I closed my eyes and let the tears fall. It wasn't his fault. I never meant to blame him. What could he have done? I turned around. Miles took my now empty coffee mug and set it on the side table next to us as I buried my face into his chest. Then he wrapped his arms around me and held me tight.

His hand found my head, and I winced. He pulled back, his gaze meeting mine. "Are you hurt?"

I shrugged as I reached up my hand to my head and remembered that was the place the branch had hit me last night. "Just from the storm last night. I'll be fine."

Worry flashed in his gaze, but I shook my head and buried my hands in the hair at the nape of his neck as I pulled his lips to mine. He was hesitant at first, but then his lips fell into sync with mine. His hands found my hips and his fingertips dug into my skin as his grip deepened with the intensity of our connection.

Just when I felt like I was going to fall forever, he pulled back.

"There's something I have to tell," he said, his voice deep as he pressed his forehead to mine.

My lips were swollen and my breath heavy, but I nodded. "What?"

He pulled back, and I brought my gaze up to meet his. "That night. The one when you lost the baby." His expression turned torturous as he stared at me.

"Yeah?" I asked, fear clinging to my chest.

"I found out Clint had been cheating on you. That afternoon, I confronted him. I told him to either make it right with you or walk away." He closed his eyes. "I never thought he'd walk away."

I stared at him as his words sunk in. Realization passed over me. This man had been protecting me his entire life. First, from my mother and then from Clint. He'd always stood in the shadows and watched, making sure that I was safe. And he never asked for anything from me.

I rose up onto my tiptoes. His eyes were still closed, and just as my lips brushed his, he whipped them open. I stared at him for a moment before I closed my eyes and pulled him to meet me so I could deepen the kiss.

He was hesitant at first, but then he pulled me so close to him that I felt as if he were going to crush me. It broke my heart that he'd carried this guilt for so long. That he thought he was the reason I'd been hurt.

When the exact opposite was true.

When he pulled back, our breaths were deep and labored. He pressed his forehead to mine, and his eyes closed for a moment before he suddenly dropped to his knee.

I stepped back, watching as he reached into his pocket and pulled out a small, black velvet box.

"Miles," I whispered as he pulled the lid open.

"Shelby, will you marry me?" he asked, keeping his gaze on the ring for a moment before he glanced up.

I stared at him and then at the ring. I knew right away whose ring it was. "Gran's?" I asked as I reached out and ran my fingers along the three diamonds that my grandfather had fitted for her. One was for their wedding, one was for the birth of my mom, and the last was for the birth of their granddaughter—me.

He nodded. "She gave it to me before she died. She always knew I loved you and hoped, someday, I could give it to you." He pulled the ring from the box and held it up. "I want you now and forever. I want you to be a mother to Belle." His voice deepened. "A mother to my children. And wife to me." He held up the ring. "What do you think?"

I stared at the ring and then back to Miles. I wanted to speak, but the words just wouldn't come. So I nodded, knelt down in front of him, and extended my hand.

He slipped the ring on my finger and then wrapped me up in a hug, his lips crashing into mine. I giggled as my hands moved from his shoulders to his back and then up to the nape of his neck. I entwined my fingers in his hair as I deepened the kiss.

He pulled back for a moment only to whisper, "I love you," before his lips found mine, and we lost ourselves in that kiss, in each other, and in the happiness that would come from a future together.

I WOKE up the next morning feeling relieved but also worried. Having Sabrina and Samuel back was amazing, and knowing what was wrong with my sister meant we could finally get her help, but there was this feeling that I couldn't quite shake.

Perhaps it was worry that Shelby and Miles weren't going to figure out they were perfect for each other. Perhaps I was still haunted with the panic that raced through me when I'd walked through the door to find Sabrina gone.

Or perhaps I wasn't sure what had happened between Bash and me, not to mention Anders. My life felt like a mess. I was teetering on the edge of a cliff where one small gust of wind would send me plummeting to my death.

It wasn't a fun place to be.

I pulled off my covers and headed to the bathroom,

where I took a long, hot shower and got out feeling mostly alive. I dressed in a comfortable pair of jeans and a sweatshirt before I threw my hair up into a bun and headed out to the kitchen. I started the coffee just as there was a knock on the door.

I pulled it open to find Dad and Penny standing there with a big paper bag and a drink carrier full of coffee cups.

"Morning," I said as I stepped away from the door so they could enter.

"Morning," Penny said as she paused to give me a kiss on the cheek, and then she followed Dad into the kitchen. "Did you two sleep well?"

I yawned at her question but followed that with a nod. "Yeah."

Penny looked skeptical but then smiled. "I'm glad. Well, your dad and I are here to help, so let me know if there's anything I can do."

I gave her a thankful smile as I took the cup of coffee Dad handed me. "Sabrina awake?" he asked.

I shrugged. "I just got up."

Penny disappeared around the corner, and shortly after, I heard her knock on Sabrina's door. Dad made his way into the living room, where he turned the TV on. The sound of a news anchor filled the silent apartment.

I rifled around in the paper bag and emerged triumphant when I found a wrapped egg and cheese sandwich. I took my breakfast food and coffee into the living room. Dad was standing in front of the TV screen, staring at it.

My phone buzzed in my pocket. I shifted my coffee to the crook of my arm so I had a free hand to pull out my phone. My stomach flipped when I saw it was a text from Anders.

Anders: I'm such an idiot. I'm so sorry about the other night. I should have been there, but I wasn't. Can you forgive me?

My thoughts went back to the pub. I'd been let down by a lot of people in my life, I just hadn't thought Anders would be another name I would add to that list. But even though he had been drunk, it wasn't like he did that *after* he found out about Sabrina. He'd been relaxing after work, so could I really hold it against him?

Me: It's okay. I understand.

I paused.

Me: Meet me for lunch?

Before I got a response, Penny came into the room carrying Samuel. When he saw me, the large smile he reserved only for me spread across his lips. I slipped my phone back into my pocket and kissed my nephew on the head.

"Morning, sweetie," I said as I nuzzled his cheek.

"Sabrina is just getting a robe and will be out in a moment," Penny said before her gaze drifted over to the TV and a confused expression passed over her face.

Intrigued, I turned to see what she was looking at. I

was met with a familiar set of deep blue eyes and dark hair. Bash was climbing out of a black SUV with cameras all around him. His hair was slicked back, and he was buttoning his suit coat as his dark expression panned the group of reporters.

"Tech billionaire Alexander Torres' son, Sebastian Torres surprised everyone with his emergence after five years," the reporter was saying.

"He's back," Penny whispered.

I glanced over at her. How did she know Bash? "You know him?"

Penny glanced over at me. "Alexander's investment group owned the publishing house I used to work for. It was a huge scandal when his younger son died tragically and his older son, Sebastian"—she waved toward the TV— "disappeared. Many thought that Alexander had murdered him." She shook her head. "I guess not."

I had so many questions. I was so confused, and yet, I couldn't find the words to say any of them.

"What's he doing on the TV?" Sabrina's sudden question had us all turning to look at her. She was pointing at the TV with a confused expression.

"You know him, too?" I asked.

She nodded before she looked over at me. "That's the man. The man that found Samuel and me. That's the man that saved me."

23

CLAIRE

SWEET TEA &
SOUTHERN GENTLEMAN

IT WAS TOO EARLY in the morning to be up. I yawned as I pulled my keys from my purse, and they jingled as I slipped the master key into the lock. The sound of dogs barking in the building caused me to smile. I may be tired, but I loved my job. Working at a shelter was the most fulfilling thing I could do.

Sure, Mom hated that my job wasn't flashy or made a ton of money, but that's why she had Cassie and Jack. They were the ones that brought her joy. Clint was an embarrassment, and as for me, well I'd learned early on to fly under the radar.

It was really the only way to survive as a Hodges.

My phone chimed as I pushed into the back of the shelter and shut the door behind me. I didn't pull it out until I was in the back room and had dumped my purse into my locker. I held it in my hand as I made my way to the coffee maker and filled it up.

Once the smell filled the air, I leaned against the counter and swiped the phone on. My entire body froze as I read the message from Cassie.

Cassie: Mom fell and broke her hip. She's at the hospital. We all talked. Since you are the one without a serious job, you're the one who needs to commit to taking care of her.

I sputtered as I stared at her words. I wanted to fight back, but I knew that was in vain. Cassie was a lawyer for high profile actors, and Jack's new wife had just won an award for her work as a heart surgeon—plus it was no secret in our family that mom hated his new wife.

Taking care of abandoned dogs was much lower on their scale of importance. Plus, even if I tried to object, they wouldn't care. It was my job to take care of mom. They'd decided.

"What's going on?" Donna asked, startling me.

I glanced over my shoulder as I quickly sent off a thumbs-up emoji and turned to face her. She was twenty years my elder and the operations manager here at the animal shelter. She wasn't going to be happy, but she was always "family matters" with us. She would let me go to Harmony, even if I didn't want to.

"My mom broke her hip," I said as I followed her from the break room to her office.

Donna stopped. "Oh my gosh. Is she okay?"

I shrugged. "I'm not sure. But I'm the only one of my siblings that can go help. So is there a chance I can get a few days off?"

Donna walked behind her desk and nodded as she picked up her calendar. "I'm sure we can arrange that." She grabbed out a pen. "I'll set your absence out for a few weeks, and if you come back early, great."

I nodded. "I'm sure it'll be just a few days. My mother is an independent woman and will fight me every step of the way."

Donne chuckled. "Sounds like my mom." She set her pen and calendar down. "Where is home for you?"

I sighed as I leaned against the doorframe. "Harmony Island, North Carolina. More specifically, the Apple Blossom B&B."

***

I hope you've enjoyed reading The Shop Around the Corner. I absolutely adored finishing Miles and Shelby's story (although they aren't completely gone yet, they'll be showing up in subsequent books).

And I'm so excited to dive deeper into Abigail and Bash's romance in the next book PLUS introduce you to Claire and her relationship with Missy....plus a broken hearted hero she's going to have to face once more. Make sure you grab, Apple Blossom B&B to find out what happens next!

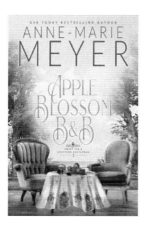

Grab it on your favorite book buying platform HERE!

Also, if you haven't read my Red Stiletto Book Club series, it's the perfect time to start! A group of women on an island form a bookclub, help each other through tough times, and fall in love with cinnamon roll heroes. Also, Abigail makes an appearance in the last 2 books!

Dive into The Magnolia Inn today!

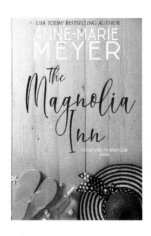

Grab it on your favorite book buying platform HERE!

Made in United States
North Haven, CT
29 August 2023

40647584R00162